An
Saga of the Stone Family

by

Sandra Garrett Salm

Sandra Garrett Salm

Printed in United States of America
Canastota Publishing Company
Canastota, NY 13032

ISBN 978-0-9766446-2-0

This book is dedicated to my mother and two sisters
who were like second mothers to me.
I miss them and love them very much

Muriel Alma Garrett Smith Morgan Fairchild
1920 - 2001

Anna Margaret Garrett Oleynick
1931 - 2008

My Mother, ~~Edna~~ *Edna* Evelyn Stone Garrett Calhoun,
was born March 1, 1899 at the Buffalo Head Hotel,
Forestport, New York. She was the oldest of thirteen
children born to Wesley and Anna Burns Stone.

While I was growing up, she insisted I have long ringlets
in my hair. To entertain me while winding my hair onto
rubber curlers at night she would share
her history of the Stone Family.

This is how I remember it.

TABLE OF CONTENTS

Chapter 1

LEAVING CANADA (1896)

"Missy. Missy, where's your ticket? I've gots to punch it," a middle-aged man was saying as she was roused out of her daydreaming. Without saying a word, she held her ticket out towards the voice. She hadn't realized how hard she had been clutching onto her train ticket. It was limp and almost torn into two pieces. The man said nothing, punched it, then handed it back. It was then that she took a moment to look up at him to see that he was a colored man. She had never seen a Negro person before and couldn't help staring at him as he proceeded to move on up the aisle. He punched each passenger's ticket as he went along.

When the colored man got to the end of the rows of seats, he disappeared. Then she saw a small wooden sign attached to the wall of the car with an arrow pointing in the same direction as the man had taken. She read the sign, "Ladies," "Now what did that mean?"

There were both men and women in the car, but since she wasn't sitting close to any of the women, she didn't feel brave enough to ask any questions. So, she turned her thoughts back to the fast-paced events of the morning.

It had seemed to her that her older brother, Peter, was taking his sweet time with the morning milking and chores. She woke up extra early and had made sure that he was up. After a quick washing in the basin of cold water, and dressing faster than usual, she carried her two carpet satchels out of the house to the waiting buckboard wagon. She spent a few extra minutes placing them where she would be able to reach them easily. Then she took a moment to look up at the sky. Seeing it was favorable, she quickly returned to the kitchen to help Momma with breakfast. She couldn't get her throat to swallow much of the hot cereal, baking powder biscuits, stewed prunes, and milky coffee. It was the same breakfast fare she'd had for as many of her sixteen years as she

1

could remember. Before today, she had eaten it automatically without much thought. But, this morning was different. This was to be her last morning sitting at this table in this house-the only one she had ever known. She dared not dwell or think about it. Somehow she forced her mind to think of what she had to do before catching the morning train.

Momma tried to get her to finish all that was in front of her because she told her daughter it might be a longer ride to America than she expected. She managed to get down most of her cereal and prunes, and drank half her coffee, but gave the biscuit to Maxey, the small family dog who sat under the table just waiting for a handout.

Peter had come in and wolfed down his share of breakfast. He was trying to enjoy a second cup of coffee when she interrupted him and urged him to please hurry. "Drats" he said. He got up, grabbed his hat, put on an old worn, but clean, top coat and went out the back door.

Momma helped her with her hat. It was a black hat with a face veil, she pinned it to her hair with two long pins. Momma said, "Hope these pins keep your hat from leaving your head. Now you've been a fine daughter, just mind your manners and be careful. I'll be saying prayers for you, aye? Be on your way with you. Enough said."

She gave Momma a quick hug and grabbed up her black purse and small black carrying bag that Momma had filled with food for her trip. She already had on her black cloth coat with four shiny black buttons. Momma had made it last week for her 16th birthday. Momma had sewed a deep pocket on each side and placed a black glove and a handkerchief in each one.

Peter had their two horses hitched to the buckboard and was waiting to give her a hand up onto the wooden seat. When they were both settled, he disengaged the wagon's brake and saying a 'gettyup' to the horses, they were off. She gave a final wave to her

Momma, who hollered after them, "Don't forget to say your prayers."

She fought back tears and tried to concentrate by looking at everything as they traveled along. She would not let Peter see her cry. She just wouldn't!

They had to make a stop at the store in Godfrey to leave a can of fresh milk and pick up the empty can from yesterday's milking. It didn't take long for the can of milk to be weighed and Peter to get back on the wagon seat, even though it seemed like it took forever.

Peter turned the team toward Westport. When they came to the fork in the road, he had to convince the team that he did want them to go to the left instead of their usual right towards home.

The horses were working as hard as they could to pull the buckboard along the rutted and partially muddy dirt road. She held her hat with one hand and grabbed the metal side of the seat with the other but still could not stop herself from asking one more time if he was sure that they would make the train on time. She didn't want to miss it. She had made up her mind a few years ago that one day she would leave home and this was that day. She did not want to spend any more days in this area, where she might run into Charlie Culter.

Peter wasn't much of a talker and she knew how he felt about her leaving. He had voiced his opinion loud and clear the night she informed Momma and him of her intentions. She knew he didn't favor her using good money to go off to America when she could just as well live here where she had always lived. She also knew that he planned to marry her off to Charlie Culter.

Charlie was looking for a wife. She had felt his eyes upon her every Sunday at church. She had to get away before he got around to speaking to Peter about her marrying up with him, now that she had turned sixteen. She had heard it said many times – "Sixteen is when all good Irish girls should be married. Those who weren't would find themselves spinsters." It was repeated at every sewing circle she and Momma had attended. Well, not her! At least not to Charlie.

Their brother, Simon, had left home some time ago. He had found work in the Adirondack Mountains. Well, girls could leave too!

It was sad to leave Momma since Poppa died. Peter had tried to fill his shoes. She knew that Momma and Poppa had traveled to Canada from Ireland when Momma turned sixteen just after they had married. Now it was her turn to travel and find out what lay beyond the world she had lived in for her sixteen years.

She tried to absorb each tree, stone, small pond, and lake as they made the trip to the station. She was glad to be going but she couldn't stop her mind from asking, "Will I ever be back here? Will I like it in America? Will I get married? Will I ever see Momma again?" She told herself that she'd come back for a visit someday.

Then she saw it - the tall church spire on the large and beautiful St. Edward's Catholic Church. They had arrived in Westport. Peter stopped the team in front of the depot. He set the break and tied the horse reins to the post and gave it an extra tight twist to be sure that the noisy train wouldn't spook them. She didn't wait for Peter to help her off the wagon; she lifted each of her satchels out of the wagon box and set them onto the wooden platform. She worked at pressing the wrinkles out of her coat and putting on her gloves. A lady wouldn't be seen in public without covering up her hands. She checked her hat and walked through the door. She had never been inside the depot. She walked over to the small open window holding her head high, trying to appear like she knew what she was doing. Mr. Barlow was stuffing what looked like mail into a large burlap sack. She waited for him to finish tying up the bundle and look up before she spoke. She opened her purse and slid several coins onto the ledge. "I'd like a ticket to America, please."

Mr. Barlow was a bit surprised to see a young woman at the window. He wasn't really sure if he had heard her right so he asked, "Where did you want to go?" She looked him straight in

4

the eye and repeated, "I'd like a ticket to America, please." Peter came in with her two satchels. Mr. Barlow looked beyond her to Peter and asked, "Am I to sell her one ticket to America?" Peter responded by nodding his head affirmatively.

Mr. Barlow counted the cost from the coins she had put in front of him. She slipped the remaining coins back into her purse. "You hold on tight to that ticket so's you don't lose it." He came around talking more to himself then to either of them "Foolish young people. What gets into them anyway? Can't seem to stay put these days. Mark my words, young lady," he turned to look directly at her, "You'll be back. Mark my words."

Peter spoke up. "Aye, she's got her mind made up. Thinks she'll find the streets of America all gold and the stores full of milk and honey. I've an idea we'll see her back home in three months begging us to find her a husband". Mr Barlow laughed and slapped Peter on the back in total agreement.

The three of them heard a train whistle in the distance. "I've got to stop that train long enough to put you on it," said Mr. Barlow as he herded them quickly out. "You'll be riding the Brockville, Westport and Sault St. Marie Railway to Kingston. You catch the river ferry and pick up the train from there. I got to stop that train by placing this red flag out so the engineer can see it and knows we want it to stop. It's not often he picks up any passengers, especially so early in the year. Summers busier with people coming home for a visit with kin folk. Usually I just thro him the mail sack and he keeps on a goin."

Butterflies were growing bigger inside her, but she was determined not to let these two men know how scared she felt. The train got bigger and bigger as all three of them watched it approach. The noise level was gaining momentum, too. As it slowed to a stop, the steam came pouring out from underneath. Mr. Barlow stood in front of her to protect her from it.

When the train was at a complete stop, a short, stocky friendly-looking man stepped from a car saying, "What you makin' us stop for, Barlow?" Mr. Barlow took a hold of one of her arms and Peter took a hold of the other. They picked her up and set her on the steps. Peter handed her the two satchels. "Go through there, Miss." Carrying a satchel in each hand, she moved down the narrow aisle. She found an empty seat in the back. She heard the man's voice shouting, "All aboard!" She began to sit down as the train started up with a jerk. It was not a lady-like position she was thrown into. She was glad none of the other passengers saw it. She did smile to herself as she proceeded to settle herself in the seat closest to the window, and set her satchels beside her on the adjacent seat. She sighed with relief and silently said to herself, "so far, so good, aye?"

She had no timepiece and had no idea how long she sat rigidly gazing out the window. She felt safe and slowly let her body relax to sink back into the plush cushion. It was comfortable. It reminded her of the parlor chair that was used only on very special occasions. When Poppa had died, and the priest came was the last time they had used the parlor. They had gone into the parlor to freshen it up. They stayed in there only long enough to air out the room, shake the dust out of the scatter rug, dust off the top of the special stuffed chair and dust mop the walls and wooden floor. Then the door was closed.

She continued to gaze out the window, but not really seeing what was there. Thoughts were tumbling around and around inside her head. She knew Momma would have liked her to stay at home but she had not tried to stop her. Momma had helped her fill the only satchel that was in the house. Momma had also given her three handkerchiefs, an extra pair of gloves, and the black hat with the long face veil that she was wearing. Momma had told her at the time that she had no need for them herself.

Peter had surprised her with a satchel just last week. He had come home with it after helping old Mr. Peaks. Mr. Peaks needed help moving him to his daughters at Bob's Lake. Peter wouldn't take any pay. He did speak up to say they could use a satchel. Mr. Peaks gave it to him.

It wasn't customary for Peter to travel to Westport on a weekday. She knew why he wasn't upset with her for his having to do so today. He would make the most of his trip home by going to Maggie's house. Margaret Gilhooly was Peter's special gal. Whenever she teased him about getting married and ask him when it was to be, he'd just shrug it off and say, "One fine day in June." Peter wouldn't quarrel with her or anyone.

She would miss Maggie. Maggie was the gentlest and kindest person that she had ever known. It was Maggie who gave her the black cloth purse with the drawstrings to close it tight. All the money she had was in there, along with a rosary, three handkerchiefs, hair combs and hair pins.

It was Maggie who had quietly told her that she had known several people who moved to America and hadn't seen any of them come back, except for visits. Maggie had slipped some coins into her hand and then closed her fingers up. When she was alone, she counted over $2.00. It brought tears to her eyes remembering. She would always be grateful to Maggie for treating her like a sister.

The train made several stops. The sound of it as it began picking up speed each time seemed to be saying over and over in her ears, "we're moving farther and farther, we're moving farther and farther." "Well," she told herself, "this is what you've dreamed about so sit back and let it be."

The conductor came through the car announcing, "Next stop, Kingston!" She saw people getting up and leaving the car. Was she supposed to? She wished she knew what to do. Just as the butterflies were starting to come back, the conductor came through checking seats. As he approached the back where she was seated, he said, "Young lady, you must get off here. Let me see your ticket." She opened her purse and took out the ticket and held it out to him. He looked at it saying, "You haveta catch the ferry and cross the river to get on the Mohawk-Malone Railroad. You best hurry." He gave her ticket back, picked up the two satchels and hurried down the aisle with her at his heels.

She stepped down. Thank goodness her legs still worked. She had sat so rigid for so long, she felt she had to tell her legs to move. "Over there," the conductor said as he motioned for her to follow him. He handed her the satchels when they could see the river. He said he could go no further.

There was a very brisk breeze blowing. It became stronger the closer she got to the water. She hurried as fast as she could, hoping her hat would stay pinned to her head. Her two hands were full so she couldn't hold on to it.

Several people were already sitting on the wooden benches on the ferry boat. "Hurry Miss. We must be gettin' along," a thin young man said as he saw her heading down the dock. She stepped on to the narrow boards. She handed her two satchels to the young man. He set them down in the boat and turned to help her. It was an awkward step she took but thank goodness she didn't lose her balance. It was embarrassing enough to have people watching her get on board. The man asked her for fifteen cents. She fumbled to open her purse and was grateful that she had enough. He took her money and stuffed it into his pocket while he unfastened the ropes. She crossed in front of people and found a space for herself and her satchels.

This ferry ride made her more nervous than riding on the train. She braced her feet as the boat moved away from the dock. No one had prepared her for this part of the trip. She had never been in a boat before and she wasn't at all sure she ever wanted to again. Where were they going? She couldn't see any land only lots of water, as the boat began moving farther and farther from the Canadian shore line.

Were these other people scared like her? As she looked timidly through the veil she tried to catch their feelings. Those closest to her seemed to be completely at ease. She closed her eyes and prayed as she folded her hands in her lap. She could hear the water slapping against the sides of the ferry. She could feel the warm spring sunshine on her back with a gentle breeze on her face. She just sat with her eyes closed, praying, until someone excitedly said

"I see it! Land, over there, look!" She opened her eyes, adjusting them to the sunlight and she could see the shore line or at least she prayed that it was. A young man walked to the other end of the ferry. She hoped he knew what he was doing. She sure didn't want to be tipped overboard. Some people started clapping. She prayed, "Oh God, please help us to get onto dry land".

After the boat bumped against the dock, the young man fastened the ropes. Some people started to stand to ready themselves for debarking. She still sat rigid until a man near her said, "It's all right to get up. You have to move first." She gathered up her belongings". She took a few unsteady steps to reach the end of the boat. She handed her satchels out and was helped out onto the dock. While on the ferry, she had overheard a conversation between an elderly gentleman and the young steersman. She watched to see where the elderly man went. He was headed for the railway, the same as her. She followed him into the depot. Seeing a woman go towards a door marked "Ladies", she followed her. She really needed to relieve herself.

She went to the ticket booth and asked when the train to Watertown would be arriving. She had an hour to wait.

Finding a seat against the wall and seeing others eating, she felt it was all right for her to get her lunch out of her bag. Momma had made her favorite pork roast on thick slices of homemade bread. She hadn't realized how hungry she really was. She brushed the few crumbs off her lap. Leaving her satchels, she walked outside to the hand pump. She helped herself to a cool drink using the dipper that was there. She went back inside to wait. Soon a whistle was heard in the distance.

Everyone came alive and they went out the door to watch the train come down the tracks. As it came around a curve, the train seemed to go on and on. It was the longest train she had ever seen. There was an ear piercing whistle before coming to a stop at the Morristown Depot. The ticket man announced for all to hear, "Goin' south! Watertown, Lowville, Lyons Falls, Remsen, Utica!

Boarding now! Train pulls away in ten minutes!" A conductor appeared from one of the cars and let down a metal step.

This train was much more plush than the first one. It was nearly full. She managed to find an empty seat next to a child. His mother motioned for her to sit down next to the boy who was watching out his window. His mother said, "That's my Ernie. He won't be a botherin' ya any. I'll see to that, aye." The woman was holding a child on her lap with another boy sitting next to her.

All was going well. She wasn't frightened anymore. She closed her eyes and rested until the conductor roused everyone as he came through to announce that they were approaching Watertown.

She felt a bit alone when they reached Watertown and the family left. Some passengers got up and left. A few new ones got on. No one sat near her. She moved to the window seat. When she had gotten on her satchels had been taken by the porter. She hoped no one mistook hers for theirs. She couldn't do anything about it but sit back and try not to worry.

It seemed like a long time before the train was on its way south. They must've added more cars to the already lengthy train because she felt a series of jerks forward and backwards. They were moving along faster and faster now. The landscape was moving faster than her eyes could focus.

The conductor came by to punch tickets and announce that they would be arriving in Lowville in half an hour. It was a short stop, but long enough to take on several male passengers. The car was now full. Rough looking and unshaven men filled the seats. A heavily bearded man sat down next to her. She kept her face turned toward the window and was glad her veil hid her eyes. She took quick glances in the direction of the men and hoped they weren't doing the same of her. She was glad the man next to her wasn't interested in talking to her, but was joining the conversation of some of his buddies.

She overheard them say they were looking for work. They planned to get off in Lyons Falls. The more she overheard, the more intrigued she became with their talk of working in Lyons Falls. She wondered if any of them knew her brother, Simon, but she wasn't about to ask. She smiled to herself and then thought about how she and Simon, were both in America. She remembered that he had a job somewhere near Carthage. What would she be doing? As far as she knew, there were no lady lumberjacks. She'd find work. She knew she could. She had very little money and needed to find something soon.

The conductor came around to punch tickets and informed everyone that the next stop was Lyons Falls. She looked out the window and saw the sun was getting lower in the sky. The train came to a stop. The men got up and filed out. The conductor came through saying, "Lyons Falls! One hour stop!" He stopped beside her seat, "Want to get off and stretch your legs a bit? Just be sure to be back on in one hour. That's 6:15 sharp, Missy. We take on lots of lumber here, but the train leaves on time."

She sure could do with a stretch and she was hungry too. She got up, straightened herself out as best she could, and exited the train. It felt good to walk. She was tired of riding. She spotted another ladies room sign. While in the small room, she spotted another sign:

WANTED
Good, dependable worker
Men's boarding house
Inquire with the ticket agent

She quickly took care of what she went in there to do. The ticket man was busy, getting bags out to the train. She forgot her shyness and approached him about what she had read. He was very kind and gave her specific directions to the boarding house. She wasted no time in walking there.

Chapter 2

LYONS FALL, NEW YORK

The sun was beginning to go down, but there was still light enough to see. The ticket agent had given her good directions. She had headed out the depot door almost before hearing them in detail. She walked to the end of the platform, down three steps and turned to the left. She hurried, almost running. At the"Y" in the street, she stopped. Left or right? She thought hard before selecting to go to the right. The agent had said she could not miss the large white house with long green shutters and a sign on the door.

"Emma's Boarding
Working Men Only"

She knocked on the door. No one came so she knocked harder. A husky, red headed boy opened the door just enough to stick out his head. He just looked at her. She began, "I'm looking for work, aye?" Before she could say more, he left her standing on the stoop, and disappeared inside the house. Someone with heavy steps approached the door. A large man with a thick red beard swung the door wide open. "Come in," he said in a voice that matched his size.

She stepped into a large dimly lit room filled with stuffed chairs and an assortment of end tables. The burly man continued in his booming voice, "So, yer a lookin for work are ya? Where'd ya come from?"

She didn't get to answer any questions because she started to feel faint and she fell. The man caught her before she hit the floor. He half dragged and half carried her over to the nearest chair. He shouted, "Emma, bring some of them smeller salts."

A short, stocky woman came limping into the room "Whatja need smelling salts fer?" Then, she saw her husband leaning over a young gal.

"Who's she?"

"Don't know," he said. "She jest started to fall. Here! Give'm ta me." He took the small bottle, opened it and passed it back and forth under her nose.

She opened her eyes and saw the two strangers standing over her. It came back to her. Feeling mighty embarrassed, she struggled to her feet.

"I'm looking for work. I saw your notice at the depot."

Emma spoke up, "Do ya know how to help around the kitchen? That's what I needs the most."

The man interrupted, "Whar ya from? Did ya jest get offa the train? We heard it pull in jest a might ago. Are ya a runnin away from something?" She was about to answer when she heard a clock chime, and remembered about the train leaving on time.

"Could you tell me the time, aye?"

Emma spoke up, "It's jest 5:30 p.m. and I's gots ta get back to the kitchen."

"I need work. I'm not running away. My Momma and Peter know I came to America. I've got to get my satchels. They are on the train."

Emma nodded her head up and down at her husband before leaving for the kitchen. She left him with the final decision. She had to see to her cooking. He took a minute to think as he ran his hand through his beard. He knew his wife was in need of help. He gave a tug on his beard and said, "I guess we'll be givin ya work. But, ya gots to help Emma. Now, wait here. Johnny will go wids ya back to the train."

The same boy, who had come to the door, came carrying a lighted lantern. She followed as he walked past her out the door. Neither of them said a word. Johnny walked at a fast trot. She was nearly breathless when they reached the depot. Johnny sat down on the bench outside the depot as she hurried inside. No one was in there. She backed out, starting to panic. Johnny followed her with the lantern a she looked under and in between each train car. They could hear voices further down the track and headed towards them. Men were busy loading lumber onto a flatbed car. She tried getting their attention by waving her arms back and forth, but they didn't seem to see her. Then it happened. Johnny had set the lantern down on the ground and putting his fingers in his mouth, he let out a shrill whistle. They all stopped for a minute until they saw it was just Johnny. The man closest to them yelled out as he kept right on working, "Git back! Can't ja see we got work ta git done?"

She spoke up as loudly as she could. "I need my satchels. Where's the depot man?"

The man answered by yelling back at her. Don't know nothing about satchels. Git yerself away from here." He turned his back to pick up more lumber.

They walked back towards the depot again looking under and around each car. They stepped up on the platform and a man's voice announced the departure of the train in fifteen minutes. She ran up to the man. "Please, I'm not going back on the train and I need my satchels." she pleaded with him. The ticket agent was busy tugging a heavy crate towards the train.

"I've got to get this loaded onto this here train before it leaves," he told her. Again, she tried to reason with him. "Please, sir, can't you get my satchels for me? They're all I own. I just have to have them before the train goes."

He set the crate up in the freight car, gave it a shove, and slid the door shut. "Com'on, Johnny," said. "Help me look in the baggage car for her dang satchels. We got no time to be on a search. Whatcha say they look like?"

Johnny crawled with his lantern up into the baggage car. She called up giving him a description of her two bags. Soon he emerged holding up two for her to see.

"Aye. That's them", she said.

"Now, after I git this train a goin' down the tracks, give me yer ticket, Miss." The ticket agent growled at her.

She thought. What did I do with my ticket? Then she remembered that it was inside her purse and her purse was at Johnny's. She and Johnny stood watching the noisy train disappear down the track before going in the depot. The agent was already busy marking boxes that had arrived.

"Thank you for my satchels," she said to him. "My ticket is in my purse at Johnny's. Could I bring it to you tomorrow?"

He shook his head up and down as he continued his work. She and Johnny left, walking at that fast trot of Johnny's.

The wall lamps had been lit inside the boarding house. Men were occupying chairs in the room as she and Johnny came through the door. Without saying a thing to any of them, she picked up her purse that she found lying on an end table. She followed Johnny out of the room. One of the men jokingly said, "Hey Johnny! Ain't ya goin' ta introduce yer girlfriend?"

Johnny completely ignored the comment. He led her through a spacious dining room with a long table all set for a meal. They went up some stairs, down a hall, and past several closed doors. She stayed close on his heels. He stopped, opened a door. He set her satchels inside and took time to light the oil lamp for her before he disappeared.

She took a moment to survey her surroundings. There was a neatly made bed that took up one wall. In front of her was a window with white curtains and a shade halfway pulled down. Next to the window was a three-drawer wooden dresser with a mirror hanging over it. There were a few wooden pegs along the wall, and a white wash bowl and pitcher were on a stand along the wall to her left. The open door took up the rest of the space. This was her first home in America.

She took off her coat and hung it on the hook she found behind the door. She set her purse and hat on the dresser. She took off her traveling dress and her shoes. She rummaged in her satchel for a work dress and her every-day shoes. She drew the dress over her head and buttoned it up the front. She put on the well worn shoes. Her feet ached but she had no time to think about that right now. She gave her hair a quick brushing, repined it, and used her hand to push that special wave in the front as best she could. "That will have to do for tonight," she said softly to herself.

Blowing out the lamp, she closed the door. Feeling along the dark hallway, she walked towards the stairs. Light shining up from the dining room let her know where the top of the stairs were. It was easy to find the kitchen. Her nose picked up delicious smells. She could hear Emma giving orders. Emma's family was helping by carrying large, heaping dishes of food out to the table. Emma handed her a dish to carry. Before she could move, Emma took hold of her arm to stop her. "What's yer name?" she asked.

"Anna. Anna Burns." Anna had been practicing her answer to that question all day so she was prepared. How she had hated her real first name, Bridget. She was starting new. Her name from now on was Anna.

Emma continued to hold her back from moving. "Wher're ya from?"

Anna answered, "Westport. Westport, Ontario, Canada."

"We gots some boarders here, come from Canada. I'll introduce ya." With that Emma led Anna into the dining room.

Chapter 3

FIRST DAY IN AMERICA

Emma suggested she go to bed when the last pan was put away. That suited Anna. It had been a long day. She finished emptying the two satchels. When she finished, she pulled back the coverlet to find two wool blankets and under them a flannel sheet. While settling herself into bed, she began to reflect on the last few hours. Emma had introduced her around the table. Emma's husband was John, their son was Johnny, and they had two girls, Clarissa who was seven, and Sarah who was six. She couldn't remember the names of all eight boarders. Anna was bone tired from the top of her head to her very sore feet. She drifted into a deep sleep with a smile on her face. She was in America. She had found work. Her name was Anna.

Someone was knocking on her door. At first she thought the sound was in her dream but as it continued, she opened her eyes. She heard Clarissa's quiet voice calling her name. "Anna, Anna are you awake?" She answered and Clarissa said, "Momma is wanting you in the kitchen." "I'll be right there," Anna answered as she stepped onto the cold floor. Last night she forgot to bring any water so she couldn't wash. She dressed quickly in the still dark room. She let the shade part way up the window and with the beginnings of daylight she was able to fix her hair.

Anna hurried down the stairs and walked through the dining room. She was glad the girls had helped her set the table for breakfast. Emma was giving Sarah a tongue lashing because the young girl had spilled quite a large amount of brown sugar on the floor. Anna took an apron from the hook and tied it around her small waist. She helped Sarah clean up her mess. Clarissa was busy getting the cereal bowls ready for Anna to dish up the hot oatmeal. Anna carried the tray of steaming bowls to the tables, while Clarissa placed one at each place, and Sarah carried the plate of warm corn muffins. Anna finished piling the sausage patties onto a platter while Emma cooked the eggs. Anna could hear the men setting themselves down to the table. She hurried with the coffee pot. It was up to her to be sure the men had plenty of hot coffee. Unlike supper, the womenfolk would eat after the men had left for work. Johnny ate with his father and had left with him. Anna found out that Johnny helped drive the horses, and helped his father with deliveries. They took meat, eggs, cheese, milk, and baked goods to various homes around Lyons Falls. At times they didn't get back home until late at night.

It was so quiet in the house after all the men were gone. Emma said it was her favorite time of the day. She called it her 'thinking' time. She would plan out the rest of her day as she sat and enjoyed her breakfast. Usually her supper was interrupted to get bowls refilled, but she hoped Anna could do that so she could sit and enjoy supper with her family.

Clarissa and Sarah had left to walk to school. Emma talked her plans out loud so Anna would know what to expect. Emma explained how she worked her week. She had three days for baking, one day for washing clothes, one day for ironing and mending, one for cleaning with Sunday for church and visiting. When Anna got the chance, she asked Emma a question she had had on her mind since last night. Anna asked, "Can Johnny talk?" Emma laughed, "Oh, yes. He can talk good as you and me but for some reason, known only to him, he picks and chooses when. I guess he started to be like that whilst he was in school." Anna then asked, "How old is he?" Emma replied, "just turned fourteen. He's been done with schoolin'. He prefers to be with his Poppa and to drive the horses. He gits to travel. He's a real good boy." Then Emma got up saying, "We'd better git us a goin'. Fore ya know it, them men will be a waitin' fer supper." She looked straight at Anna and asked her, "Could ya git up outa bed earlier? I needs ya ta put up the dinner pails." Anna answered by saying 'aye'. She had heard the men picking up pails as they went out the door. She had not realized it till this moment that Emma must have gotten up real early and filled the men's pails before she started breakfast. Emma was sure a worker. Anna liked her and wanted to help to do her share of the work.

Today was wash day. Anna was sent upstairs to gather up the piles of dirty wash the men had left to be picked up. Emma told Anna about Lyons Falls as they worked. It was a lumber town. The railroad had given a big boost to the town. New workers came all the time, and easily found some kind of work usually either for the saw mills or the paper mill. The town had a doctor, a fire hose company, several churches, a livery stable, dress makers, hat store, bakery, mercantile, and a school with two rooms. One room for her girls till they completed third grade and a second room for the older children up to the eighth grade. Most left school after sixth grade. They had to attend the academy in Lowville or in Boonville and be boarded out with families. Most families couldn't afford the cost of having their son not helping at home. Anna was picturing each place as Emma talked. She hoped she'd get to walk to see all of them. Anna was reminded that she had to send a letter home when Emma described the post office. Emma said she would loan Anna some paper and ink until she could get to the mercantile to buy her own.

She wrote a letter to Momma letting her know that she was fine. It was a sunny day but still cold with the wind blowing. She was glad for her warm coat and gloves. She pinned the veil up on top of her hat. She took a leisurely walk up the street to the post office. Emma had told her Mr. and Mrs. Thompson ran the post office out of one room in their house. The railway depot, being close by, made it easy for the Thompsons to send and receive the Lyons Falls mail. Mr. Thompson was delivering mail around town so Anna didn't get to meet him. When she had knocked on their house door, Mrs. Thompson had welcomed her and told her in the future not to knock but enter and ring a bell on the desk. Anna purchased an envelope and paid Canadian postage for her letter. She was assured it would be on the next train going north.

Anna was drawn to this friendly, gray haired lady who smiled all the time. Mrs. Thompson asked Anna to sit down to have a cup of tea. Mrs. Thompson was familiar with hearing about Canada since there were many Canadian men working in Lyons Falls. She kept a ready supply of Canadian stamps on hand. She often helped address envelopes for the men when they sent money back to their families. Anna wanted to stay longer and keep visiting but when she opened her purse to pay for the stamp, she saw her train ticket and remembered she had to take it to the ticket agent. She didn't know what he wanted it for, but she had said she would bring it today. She intended to keep her word. She said goodbye to Mrs. Thompson, who told her to come and visit anytime.

When she reached the depot, she didn't see anyone inside. She was about to leave when she heard a snore coming from the other side of the ticket window. Anna looked through the window and saw the ticket agent sleeping on a cot. Just as she was deciding not to disturb him, but come back another day, she heard a train whistle some distance away. Immediately the man jumped to his feet. He slapped his train cap on his head. It was then he saw her watching him through the small window. "Change yer mind 'bout staying here?" He asked. "No," she answered "I brought you my ticket."

"So ya did, "he said. "Well, let's have a looky at it." After studying it a while, he said, "Ya gots some money a comin ta ya." She had a puzzled look on her face, so he explained. "This here ticket was ta take ya ta Utica. That's further south. Since ya got offa here in Lyons Falls, yer gots money comin ta ya." He did some figuring on a piece of paper. He opened a drawer below the window and said, "Hold out yer hand." Into her gloved hand, he dropped several coins. She was surprised and smiled as she thanked him. She had best hurry and get back to Emma's. She felt like skipping as she went, but thought better of it. She was a working lady now, not a silly child anymore. She felt very happy and rich. In one day, she had found work, had a room of her own, and money in her purse. Anna liked America.

Giving up the name Bridget felt right, just like her decision to make a new life in America. For her first ten years of life she hadn't minded being called Bridget. She had been told many times that she was named for Grandma Burns.

But, after accidentally overhearing the argument between Momma and Grandma Burns, Anna had hated her name. That day she had learned the truth. No one had ever told her that she wasn't really a "Burns." Her natural mother had left her with Mary and Peter Burns who had five boys. Momma and Poppa, Peter and Simon had treated her as part of the family. The other three boys she didn't remember. They were grown and had left the area.

She was expected to do all kinds of chores for Grandma Burns who lived alone some distance away. Grandma Burns couldn't get around very well but she sure could hit with that cane of hers. Whenever she didn't think things were done well enough or for just any reason it seemed to Anna she'd hit her with that cane. Anna was ashamed of herself for being glad the day Poppa had found Grandma had died in her sleep.

Chapter 4

JACK

The vegetable garden was beginning to grow. Anna was glad the family had asked her to help them plant and weed it. After supper, all of them spent the remaining daylight out there. It was large so every hand was needed. Often, several of the boarders came out and worked. The peas, lettuce and radishes would be ready first. She and the girls liked to watch the beans sprout like rows of tiny umbrellas coming out of the ground. There were poles for them to climb on. The cucumbers also had poles but it would take longer for them to climb. It would even be longer for them to be big enough to make into pickles. Everyone was anxious to eat the tomatoes, but they would take most of the summer. In a separate plot, the corn had been planted along side many long rows of potatoes and winter squash. Clarissa and Sarah checked everyday to see if the corn was ready. They could hardly wait to have corn on the cob. Anna knew they were in for quite a wait.

There were plenty of potatoes to hill up and carrots to keep weeded. Anna wasn't crazy about doing it but she did enjoy working outdoors. Anna had plenty of practice caring for potatoes, as Poppa and Momma raised them every year. They would tell her about how there had been a terrible blight. It affected every family. It was a struggle for families to feed themselves. That's why they decided to get on a ship coming to Canada soon after they married. Hundreds of others came at the same time. Most found work building the canal, near Westport. It was hard work, but there was land and they could raise their own food. Anna had to fight back tears if she let her mind drift to life at home. She missed Momma. She wondered how Momma was doing.

The flowers were planted around the house in various places. It seemed for a long time that they weren't going to have any flowers, but all of a sudden, after a soaking rain, the green stems began to appear. Emma and Anna watched for the first blossoms. Momma loved to have a glass of flowers on the table. Anna had spent her carefree hours searching the woods and meadows for wild flowers. How Momma's face would light up whenever Anna came in the house carrying a handful.

The week days passed quickly. There was always lots to do to fill each day, but Sunday afternoons were very lonely. After an early breakfast, she would dress in her 'Best' dress and shoes, put on her hat with the veil to cover her face, and her gloves. She would then walk to the Catholic Church. If it was raining, she would borrow an umbrella from Emma. She sat with the Thompson's. If they weren't invited to someone's house for Sunday dinner, they would invite her to join them for a simple, cold meal. She did enjoy both of them and was grateful for their kindness to her.

Emma and John attended another church. They usually went visiting one of their relatives in the area. It really was the only time they had to spend time together away from the house as a family. They invited Anna to go with them, but she never did. She felt she intruded enough in their lives.

There was another reason Anna gave them this time without her. The Thompson's had a library of books. Anna was encouraged to borrow them. She did love to read. The little schooling she had had was enough to teach her to enjoy reading. She would put herself into the story and forget where she was, or how homesick she felt. Sunday became her 'reading' day. On sunny, warm days, she took a coverlet and spread it out on the ground. That is, until Jack moved into the boarding house.

Anna would not forget the first time she laid eyes on Jack. He came home one evening with the men. He was so brazen. He came walking right into the kitchen, took hold of Emma's hand and kissed it. He asked her if he might have a room in her fine establishment. He was a charmer. Emma was flattered. He moved in that very night. Anna had been asked to show Jack his room. He had followed her and then, he invited her to come to his room anytime. She hurried herself back down the stairs. All during his first meal and every meal after that, she could feel his eyes following her around the room. Anna couldn't help feeling attracted to him. His charming ways were hard to ignore. At the same time, she felt so uneasy whenever he was around.

Jack was boastful with the men. He was always telling stories. Each story made him look smart or strong. The men laughed at his stories, knowing they were made up. Jack put a spark into their otherwise routine lives. Some times he used language not suitable for young ears. She had seen John take Jack off to the side to remind him to be more careful when talking in the house.

Anna usually only saw Jack at breakfast and supper. He like the other boarders went elsewhere on weekends. Anna was told the lumberjacks liked to drink and no one was allowed to use or have liquor in their rooms or to come home drunk. Well, she had no idea where they spent their Sundays, nor did she care to know.

Saturday night there were dances at the Town Hall. She went with Emma, John and the three children. Some of the boarders also were there.

Anna looked forward to those dances. She had so much fun. From the moment they got there, she was on the floor dancing. Being a lumber town, men outnumbered women so there was no lack of male partners. If no one asked her to dance, Johnny would be right there. He seemed to enjoy dancing as much as she did. She felt safe and happy there because John was one of three big men who watched and made sure all went well. More than once, she had seen John escort a man out who was drunk, rude or trying to start a fight.

Each week, she had seen Jack at the dances. She had caught him looking at her but, he had never asked her to dance. She noticed he didn't really do much dancing. He mostly stood around watching and talking with the other men who stood off to the side. She sometimes had seen Jack walk a girl outside. One night when she found herself near him, he asked her very politely if she would care to walk outside to get some fresh air. She told him she had to help with the refreshments. She tried to keep herself busy and away from him. Two weeks later, Anna's life changed. Jack was at the dance. He claimed it was his birthday. The fiddler played and everyone sang 'Happy Birthday' to Jack. This particular Saturday night, John and Johnny had not gotten back from making their deliveries. Emma had driven Anna and the girls to the dance with their spare horse and wagon. Anna could feel Jack's eyes on her and it seemed he never took them off her.

Anna accepted dance partners readily but did her best to stay away from where Jack was standing. A bit later Clarissa begged Anna to go out to the privy with her. Anna tried to get Clarissa to ask her mother or one of the other older girls to go out with her. Clarissa insisted that only Anna go with her. Anna did see that Emma was busy fixing the sandwiches and setting them out along with the lemonade to have during the musicians break time. Anna finally gave in when Clarissa said she couldn't 'hold it' any longer. They went outside and around the building to the ladies privy. It was a two holer so Anna went in with her.

Jack was right there to greet them when they came out. He told Clarissa her mother needed her and she was to hurry. Anna tried to duck around him. She tried going under his arm. He grabbed one of her arms and put his other hand over her mouth as he pulled her behind the privy. She tried to free herself from his grip. She swung her free arm at him, but he was much stronger than her. He pushed her up against the small building. He pressed his body up against hers. He reeked with the odor of whiskey. He said he just wanted a Happy Birthday kiss from her. He took his hand off her mouth, but before she could get a sound out, he had his mouth on hers. He grabbed her free arm holding both of her arms behind her. She struggled to get loose. He held her so tightly that she couldn't breathe. He kept his mouth on hers and she went limp.

A shrill whistle came from behind Jack. As he turned just a bit to find out what the sound was all about, he loosened his grip on Anna. She fell in a heap to the ground. Johnny punched Jack in the gut. Jack doubled over and Johnny began hitting him on the head and in the face. Jack fell on the ground. Johnny kicked him several times as Jack tried to roll away from him. John came then. He grabbed his son away from Jack.

"That's enough, Johnny. Stop!"

Johnny went to see how Anna was. He helped her to her feet. She was sobbing. He handed her his handkerchief. She wiped her eyes. John had gotten Jack to his feet and handed him over to some other men. John asked Anna if she was hurt. Through her tears she answered, "No." John told his son to help Anna to their wagon and to stay with her.

"I'll go git yer Ma and the girls. Ya drive them home. I'll be along later".

Johnny took Anna by the arm and helped her to the wagon. His mother and sisters came running. "Are ya hurt, Anna?" asked Emma. "No." replied Anna.

The girls climbed up in the back of the wagon. One sitting on either side of Anna and each holding one of Anna's hands.

Anna was ever so glad to finally be alone in her room. She washed her face and scrubbed her lips till they were raw. Then she got into bed and cried herself to sleep.

Chapter 5

GO OR STAY?

Anna didn't sleep well that night. She spent most of the dark hours sitting on the edge of her bed. She couldn't keep her body from shaking. She felt so cold that she put her coat on for warmth. The coat reminded her of Momma and at this moment she'd give anything to be back home, letting Momma hold her and rocking her in her own room. When the first rays of light appeared in the eastern sky, Anna washed her face, dressed, pinned her hair on top of her head, and went downstairs. No one was up yet.

She sat in the kitchen, rocking and rocking. She had no idea for how long. She had a nice, warm fire going in the cook-stove by the time Emma came down to make breakfast. Anna was glad for something to do. While they prepared the meal together, Emma told Anna that John had come home very late. He had made sure Jack was taken away by the sheriff. He would be put on the next train going west. Emma did her best to reassure Anna that Jack would not ever bother her again. He would be told never to come around here again. Anna wanted so much to believe her, but, it was hard right now.

This was Sunday. That meant the boarders would not be back until after dark tonight. She didn't want to see any of them.

She helped Emma with the breakfast dishes then she dressed for church, making sure the veil on her hat was far down over her face. She walked to the Thompson's as fast as she could, looking behind her from time to time. She knew it was early but she wanted to ride to church with them. She didn't want to walk into church this morning by herself. Once in church, she felt safe and her stomach stopped churning. Church was one place Anna was sure that Jack would not be. When church was over, she accepted the Thompson's invitation to dinner. She felt very safe in their house. The Thompson's were glad for company and they enjoyed telling her about themselves. Listening to them, kept her mind off her fears. She stayed later than usual. In fact, so long that Emma sent Johnny looking for her.

Anna didn't sleep much that night either. She did try. But, when she closed her eyes, she was filled with fears. The covers on top of her reminded her of Jack smothering her with his body. She thought she heard noises out in the hall that might be Jack creeping up to her room. Her mind played tricks on her. She fought hard to think of happier times. Fun times she had had growing up. She missed Momma, maybe, she should forget about living here in America and go back home. She let the tears fall onto her pillow.

She must have fallen asleep because the next thing she knew, Clarissa was calling softly to her. She answered that she'd be right down.

That morning, she stayed in the kitchen and handed the breakfast food to Clarissa and Sarah to carry to the table. Emma sensed her reluctance to leave the kitchen, so she poured the coffee. Anna didn't want the men to look at her with their accusing, all knowing looks. How would she ever face them, knowing they would blame her for what happened.

As usual, Emma had a full day planned for both of them. Anna worked even faster than Emma could come up with work to be done. In fact, Anna even had extra time to work out in the garden. She picked up the hoe, pretending that each weed she found was Jack. She dug at it with a vengeance. She was determined to be rid of Jack. By the time she reached the end of each long row, she was feeling better and better. A song began to come forth from her mouth. She quietly hummed to herself.

Just then the girls came bounding up to her. They were full of exciting news. Both were going to be in a school play. They wanted Anna to help them memorize their parts. They went on and on about school as they walked back to the house.

Emma again poured coffee for the men at supper. Anna carried dishes of food out to the tables. Then hurried back to the safety of the kitchen. When out at the tables, she avoided looking at any of the men, but to her surprise, none of them seem to even notice her. All through the meal, no one spoke of Jack or the incident.

As the days passed, the nights got a bit easier and Anna began to sleep without much trouble. One afternoon, as Anna and Mrs. Thompson were enjoying tea together, Anna told her about her fears and how she couldn't decide whether she should stay here, or go back to Canada. It was then that Mrs. Thompson remembered Mr. Thompson telling her that during his last trip to Boonville, he had heard that the Hulbert House was looking for help. She went on to tell Anna about the Hulbert House. She told her how it was the largest and finest hotel in Boonville and probably best in the state of New York. That it was built in the early 1800's and had had famous people stay there. It had a fine reputation and Anna shouldn't worry about working there. If she wanted to, Anna could ride there with Mr. Thompson on his next trip. Anna was interested, but told her she needed to think about it.

She did a great deal of thinking about it. All the next week, as she pulled weeds in the garden she thought about it. She prayed to God for an answer. Should she go back home or should she stay here in America. One day she felt a peace come over her. She decided she would go to Boonville. The hardest part was to tell the family. They had been so good to her. She would miss each one of them.

John and Emma wished her well and said they understood her decision. Johnny said nothing. He just left the room. Clarissa and Sarah cried and clung to her, begging her not to leave. But she had made up her mind, and wasn't about to change it.

The early morning drive with Mr. Thompson was enjoyable. He was a careful driver who spoke gently and quietly to his team. The two horses were named Gilly and Spook. He had owned them a long time. Gilly was named after the family he worked for years ago. Spook, he named, after the way he had gotten him. Spook was traveling with several other horses by train from somewhere in Pennsylvania up to the Adirondack Mountains to be used in the woods. Mr. Thompson told her that the train had derailed on a curve just before reaching Lyons Falls. The car carrying the horses tipped onto its side. Some of the horses died when others fell on top of them. Spook was one of the lucky ones. When the car door was slid open, Spook jumped out and ran. Mr. Thompson joined other area men to catch him. All the other men gave up after two days of hunting. Mr. Thompson was determined to keep on trying. Every day he would take some hay and some grain out to where Spook had last been seen. He would sit quietly hoping to get close to him when he came to eat but Spook kept away. The food was gone the next morning when Mr. Thompson came back. It took time, but Mr. Thompson was patient. Spook came to trust him. Soon Mr. Thompson was able to get a rope around his neck and lead him home. He was able to purchase Spook for a small amount of money. It all worked out as Gilly and Spook made a fine working team.

Mr. Thompson had always lived around Lyons Falls and he told her stories about how it used to be when he was a youngster. Time flew by and soon Mr. Thompson said they were nearing Boonville.

Anna thought, Well, here I am in another new town. What will I do now? Maybe I should just go back and work in Lyons Falls. Anna began praying to herself. God, please help me to find a new home and work to pay my way. I really don't want to go back to Canada and hear everyone say –"I told you you'd be back with your tail between your legs". Oh, God, I really do want to stay in America. Please help me, aye?

Chapter 6

BOONVILLE

The sun was high in the sky and shining brightly when Mr. Thompson and Anna arrived in Boonville. The two horses had had a fairly easy time pulling the carriage up and down the rolling, rutted dirt roads. There had only been a few scattered farms to gaze at over the several miles they had covered this morning. Now Anna could tell they were coming into a town because the houses were built side by side along both sides of the village plank road. They crossed over several other streets lined with houses. She would have a lot to write and tell Momma. This was the largest town she had ever been to in her life.

They circled around an area of grass called a park with roads going away from it in every direction. Mr. Thompson directed the team to stop along the board side walk. He secured the horses to the hitching post and helped Anna out of the carriage. Anna used her hands to press wrinkles out of her best Sunday dress. She checked her hat and put on her gloves. Mr. Thompson had her satchels in his hands and told her to take a hold of his arm. As she raised her eyes to see where they were headed, she saw a very tall brick building across the street. She read the sign – Hulbert House and above the name, the year 1812. Mr. Thompson had taken a step off the boards saying, "Come along, Anna. Let's go find you a place to stay and some work."

It nearly took her breath away. She had never seen such a fine place. She prayed a silent prayer as they crossed the street and prepared to enter the front door. "Oh God, I hope to work here. Please let it be possible."

She had only a moment to notice the first room. There was a high desk and behind it on the wall were small boxes, some empty and some with keys. Mr. Thompson hustled her ahead of him into a spacious dining room. Her eyes took in the beauty of this room. She hadn't finished looking it all over when a nice looking woman entered from a side door. She introduced herself as Caroline Alexander. Mr. Thompson introduced himself and Anna. He did all the talking. Anna stood captivated by the beauty of the room. When he had explained why they were there. Mrs. Alexander said she was the cook but if they would remain there, she would fine Mr. Simcourt, the owner.

They didn't have to wait long. Mr. Simcourt looked Anna up and down while Mr. Thompson told what a fine girl Anna Burns was and how he knew she would be a dependable worker. Did he have any openings? Mr. Simcourt answered that as a matter of fact he was looking for a second waitress. He addressed Anna asking her if she could do that kind of work. "Aye." Anna answered with a smile as she took his hand to shake it. He replied that he would give her a try on the recommendation of his good friend. He excused himself and soon came back with a young girl that Anna judged to be about her own age. She was asked to help Anna with her belongings. Mr. Thompson said he had to leave for he had an appointment down the street. He squeezed Anna's hand as he said goodbye saying they would be looking for a letter telling them how she was doing. Anna promised.

Each girl took a satchel. Anna followed as she was led upstairs and down a long hallway. They walked all the way to the end stopping just before a door leading to an outside stairway. Anna would be sharing this room with Flora Bellinger. She liked Flora immediately. She had a big, friendly smile, and a quiet easy laugh and a quick step as she walked. Flora seemed to be a very happy person.

Flora was a chatterbox. From the moment they left the dining room, she began talking to Anna as if they had known each other all their lives. Anna felt safe and comfortable already. It would be a new experience for her to have another girl to share a room and a bed with. Flora squeezed Anna's hands and told her she was glad to have her there.

Anna took off her hat and dress and put on her second best dress and her only other pair of shoes. "Are ya hungry?" Flora asked

Anna. "Aye" Anna answered. "We'll eat now, and while we eat, I'll tell you what you have to do". They went down to the kitchen. She had already met Mrs. Alexander who was busy at the sink. Flora looked around for Big Tommy but he wasn't around. Oh well, she'd introduce Anna to him later. Flora showed Anna where the dishes, cups, and utensils were kept. She had not realized how very hungry she was until she smelled the food. They sat at a table in a side dining room. Flora explained everything. How serving dinner was different from serving supper and breakfast. Anna was having a hard time keeping up with all she was hearing but Flora told her not to worry that she would help. Flora said it was going to be so much fun having Anna here. She gave Anna a quick tour of the dining rooms at the hotel. Anna especially liked the small one that had its own fire place. Now, it was time to wait on the guests. Flora handed her an apron. Anna had pinned her hair up off her face. They were never to serve people with their hair down about their face or on their shoulders. Anna stood and watched Flora. She admired how Flora was friendly with each guest.

After dinner they had a couple of hours to themselves. Flora asked her, "Would ya care to see the town or are ya hankering to have a nap?" Anna said she'd love to get outside and walk. It would do her legs good. They were still feeling stiff after the long ride from Lyons Falls.

"Let's see, Whar shall we go first?" Flora was asking more to herself than to Anna. "I know. We'll go to see if John is around." "Who's John, aye?" asked Anna. "Oh," giggled Flora." He's just about the best looking man I ever met." Then she continued in a low whisper, "I sure hope he'll git around to asking me to marry him." That began a whole lot of chatter from Flora about John. How they met at a dance last year, how she tries to find time to see him whenever he's not out delivering and on and on she talked. Then she stopped, saying "Here it is. John works here for the livery. He delivers all kinds of goods all over the area. Who ever needs somethin' taken or picked up, my John's the one ta do it. He told me he's saving money so he can have his own farm someday." Anna could hear the pride in her voice. They stepped inside the livery. It smelled like sweet hay. No one seemed to be around.

"We'll see him later" she said as she turned around and led Anna on down the street. They hurried right along so she could show Anna several of the stores……..She went on to inform Anna that she couldn't afford to buy any of the fancy hats or dresses but she enjoyed looking at things and feeling the material. Flora went up one street and down another, weaving here and there. It was a bit confusing to Anna just where they were but she was enjoying herself. Her fears had been forgotten and her stomach was no longer full of twinges.

That night as they lay in bed talking Flora told Anna about everyone who worked at the hotel. Mr. Simcourt's wife had died some years back. Caroline Alexander was a widow with two girls. Effie and Lydia Arabella, to raise. They lived on North Street. Mrs. Alexander walked to work each day. She had been the cook for several years now.

Big Tommy was a mystery. He didn't talk about himself and stayed in his room there in the hotel when he wasn't working in the kitchen. He did all the baking. Big Tommy was a large, tall black man with big black eyes that seemed to snap at you along with his quick temper. It was wise to jump when he asked you to do something. She knew that there were Delores and Mary. They cleaned the rooms and did the laundry. Downstairs there was a saloon room. It had its own front entrance but you could get there from a side door in the hotel lobby. Flora had never been in there but once when the door was open she looked in. She saw men standing up to the bar holding glasses of drink. The room reeked of cigar smoke and was dimly lit. Whatever Flora went on talking about that night, Anna did not hear. She was sound asleep.

CHAPTER 7

BERRYING

"Oh, thar ya are. I've been alookin all over for ya. Want ta go berrying with me, tomorra?" asked Flora. She had found Anna out back of the hotel sitting on a blanket with her back braced against a large maple tree. Ever since Anna had found the Library in Boonville, she spent her spare time reading. Anna loved being outdoors on sunny days, especially when she had a book to read. She had discovered this especially nice shade tree where there always seemed to be a breeze to cool off the hottest part of the day. Anna had been so absorbed with her reading that she had not heard what Flora said to her. Anna took her eyes off the page and looked up and asked, "aye?"

"Oh, you are always reading a book! I really don't see what ya like about all that reading ya do." Flora said in an exasperating tone of voice. She had known Anna long enough to know she had probably not heard her. She really liked Anna but she just could not understand this part of her. So, Flora asked again. "I asked ya if ya wanted ta go pickin berries with me tomorra on our day off? Ya been aworkin here several weeks and haven't even been outa town. Well, what ja say?"

Anna answered with another question. " Where, aye?" Flora answered, "Over in Forestport. John said we could hitch a ride with him 'cause he'll be making deliveries." She went on, "We have ta be ready ta leave at first light. C'mon. I really wants ya to go. It'll be fun ta get away from here."

Anna took her eyes from Flora and looked beyond her friend. Flora was right. She had not been out of Boonville or even far from the hotel since she had come. She hesitated a moment longer, before giving an answer. She really had planned to finish reading the rest of this book. She could do that if she was here, but, on the other hand it might be fun to get away. She had heard only good things said about Forestport and the Buffalo Head Hotel over there.

Maybe they'd drive past it. She'd never know if she didn't go. Anna nodded her head up and down. Flora began jumping up and down. She swung her arms up over her head with a kind of war dance and she spun around on her heels and ran back towards the hotel, saying as she ran, "I'll talk ta ya about it later." Anna sat for the next minute thinking about tomorrow. Then, she settled her back again against the tree trunk and resumed her reading.

Flora and Anna didn't get time to talk about their plans until they had finished up washing and drying the last of the cooking pots that evening. Flora had it all planned out. She had gotten permission from Big Tommy to borrow a large kettle with two handles and two small pails. They would carry a quart tin milk can filled with drinking water and she had made each of them a thick meat sandwich. She tied the sandwiches inside her apron.

They headed for bed right after the last pan was put away. There'd be no sitting out on the back porch tonight. Lately, Flora talked to Anna about the plans she and John were making. He had recently proposed to her. They were to be married at her grandmother's on September 28th, her grandmother's 85th birthday.

Anna did some tossing and turning before finally drifting off into a deep sleep. It seemed like she had just gotten to sleep when she felt Flora gently rocking her shoulder and whispering that it was time to get going if they were to meet John on time. They took turns splashing their faces with the cool water in the wash basin. They dressed quickly and then went down to the kitchen. They ate some left over corn cake and had a cup of milk. Flora put her apron, water can, and pails inside the kettle. It certainly was quiet outside this time of day. It was still dark with a sliver of the moon giving them enough light to see their way along the street. They both sighed a bit of relief when they found John hitching up the team outside the livery. The buckboard delivery wagon was full of feed, bags, wooden boxes and barrels. Three people couldn't sit up on the seat, so the girls would take turns. Anna let John help her up into the back. She squeezed her feet between the soft feed bags and sat down. John quipped to Anna that riding was a bit better than walking all the way to Forestport. He started right in teasing Flora the minute she got up beside him.

"You two got here just in the nick of time, 'cause I woulda been gone without ya." John said as he turned his face so they wouldn't see him grinning. "Ya wouldn't a done that and ya knows it." Flora came back with as she gave him a firm poke in the ribs.

Anna watched the sky grow lighter and lighter. She rested her back against a barrel and enjoyed the ride. It didn't take long for her to be glad she had taken Flora up on this idea. She began thinking about what she had overheard hotel guests say about Forestport and the famous eating place there—the Buffalo Head Hotel. Some said you got more to eat there that you could possibly eat at one time. She'd like to see it. When it was her turn to sit up with John, she'd ask him if they would be driving past it. She hoped so.

When John stopped to water and rest the horses, Anna changed places with Flora. She plied John with questions about Forestport. "How far is it to Forestport, aye?" John thought a minute before answering and then said, "I reckon it's the same distance going to Forestport as it is to come back from Forestport." Well, that wasn't the kind of an answer Anna wanted to hear but she forgot it because John went on talking about the times he had delivered there and about all the goods he had hauled back to Boonville. John liked to talk. He was glad to have the girls along for company. He usually drove alone unless someone hitched a ride goin' one way or 'nother. It seemed to Anna that John knew more about Forestport than he did Boonville. He sure made it sound special. Then he told them that he was born and raised there.

The sun was already well up in the sky when John announced they had reached Forestport. The horse's hooves made a different and almost musical sound as they clip-clopped across the wooden bridge over the Black River. On the other side, John stopped the team, secured the wagon, jumped off and helped each girl to get down. He told them they were on their own until late in the afternoon. He would be ready to head back to Boonville when the sun gets about there in the sky. He pointed in the direction he reasoned they would see it.

Flora had been here last year picking berries so she knew where to look for bushes. They waved goodbye to John. Each picked up a handle of the kettle and started walking off to the right. Flora didn't waste any time. They walked faster and faster until they were running. The road turned left onto a narrow dirt road that gradually turned into a foot path. Choosing a shade tree they set the kettle down and took a minute to catch their breath. After taking a sip of water, they stood the can on the ground and propped the wrapped sandwiches next to it, and then placed the kettle upside down over all. "That should keep any furry varmints from gittin our lunch," Flora quipped.

"Here, you pick in this." Flora said as she handed Anna a pail. If ya wear yer scarf, I'll be able to tell whar ya are. "I want ta know where ya are all the time. I'm afraid of wild animals especially bears. I never saw one and I don't care ta start today."

All morning they kept an eye on each other and a sharp ear for any strange sounds. Each time their pail was full, they dumped it into the kettle. When the sun was directly overhead, they decided it was time to eat. It was getting quite warm out. The shade tree felt good to stand under. There was an army of ants around so they didn't dare sit down. The water tasted good, even if it was warm, and the sandwiches hit the spot. As they ate, Anna told Flora about the baby brown bear cub she once had when she was growing up in Canada. Flora was spellbound, listening to Anna's story. Anna told how one afternoon on her way home from school, she strayed a bit off her usual way to look for flowers to pick for Momma.

She came upon a baby cub who seemed to be crying softly as she came near one of the large flat rocks she stepped on to warm her bare feet. She reached down and picked up the cub. It nestled down into her arms and she carried it home. As she walked the rest of the way home, she made a lot of great plans for her and her 'baby'. She was going to let it sit and eat at the table with her, and sleep with her at night, and she'd ask Momma if they could make it some clothes to wear. She was so full of excitement. But Momma and Poppa Burns were not happy to see her bear cub. They scolded her and said she should have left it alone. She pleaded with them to let her keep it. She promised to always take care of it. She was convinced that the cub was all alone and needed her. Finally, they gave in and let her keep it, but out in the back woodshed. It was never to come inside the house. She saved scrapes of her meals to feed, Bucky. That's what she named it. Every waking minute she could, she played outdoors with the cub. They rolled and tumbled together and ran around the trees. Her baby grew fast. One morning she got up as usual and ran to the woodshed to see Bucky. He was gone. She looked everywhere. She called and called. She questioned Poppa. She thought maybe he had run Bucky off because he never really liked him. When she asked, Poppa told her he had not seen him. She spent days trying to find him. She cried herself to sleep at night. Poppa said that Bucky was a wild animal and that he probably found another bear cub and they had run off together. Anna finally came to accept it. She began to picture in her head, Bucky with a brother or sister finding berries and running farther and farther away. She had nearly forgotten about him until today.

The girls went back to picking berries. They were both pouring berries in the kettle when Flora spoke, "Do ya feel what I feel?" Anna nodded her head yes. It was starting to sprinkle. They took off their scarves and put them over the berries, and put the apron over all. They each took a handle. The kettle was much heavier than when it was empty. Carrying it between them and walking as fast as they could without spilling it, they headed back down the path. The rain drops began falling faster. As they reached the road, Flora said, "We'd better head for cover. It's too far to the General Store, let's go this way." Anna walked along as fast as she could to keep up wherever Flora was leading them. She silently hoped Flora knew where she was going. They hurried past some houses. Flora didn't let up her fast pace until she stopped right in front of the Buffalo Head Hotel. They managed to reach the front door just as a loud clap of thunder scared both of them. Flora opened the door pulling Anna almost in on top of the kettle as she set it down just inside the door. Anna somehow stopped herself from falling. She looked up and found that they were standing on a very plush rug. Neither girl dared to take another step. They felt small and out of place with their old and now very wet clothes and shoes on this rug.

A tingling bell had rung when they had opened the hotel door. A man, dressed very neatly in a three piece suit, entered the room, saying, "Ladies, may I help you in some way?" Anna kept quiet and did her best not to stare at him. Flora spoke up for the both of them, "Sorry ta bother ya. We were just trying ta keep from getting' a soaking. We've been berrying." As she spoke she moved the cloths a bit to uncover the blueberries. Then she continued. "Could we rest here until the rain lets up a bit? We hav' ta catch our ride back to Boonville. Maybe you know John Daniels. He grew up here in Forestport. He works for the livery in Boonville. He delivers all kinds of goods here abouts. He's at the General Store today. Flora turned and pointed in the direction she thought was where John might be. Anna thought Flora was going to tell the man their whole life story before she stopped. Anna wasn't one to interrupt when someone else was speaking, but she did cut in on Flora, Anna stepped forward a bit, and started talking.

"My name is Anna Burns, aye, and this is Flora Bellinger. I've been hoping to see your hotel. I've heard wonderful things about the food you serve here. Would you be needin' another worker?" Anna had no idea what possessed her to speak out so boldly to this stranger. But as she had heard Poppa Burns say-'nothing ventured, nothing gained" what did she have to lose?

The man came over and shook their hands. "I'm William Watson. My wife, Gladys and I own the hotel. She does all the cooking and decides who works here. Are you both looking for work?" Flora shook her head no and kept quiet but sure wanted to ask Anna what she was thinking asking for a job. "Follow me and I'll introduce you to Mrs. Watson." Flora poked Anna in the side with a questioning look on her face as Anna stepped ahead of her. From the hotel lobby they followed Mr. Watson through the dining room. It was full of round tables covered with white tablecloths and set up for the next meal. Anna noticed that there was a huge Buffalo Head mounted on one wall. Then through swinging doors, thcy entered into a large kitchen.

Mrs. Gladys Watson was the opposite of her husband. She was short, frumpy, hair pulled tight into a kind of knot on her head, with an unfriendly look on her face. Anna's first thought was how do wonderful dishes of food come from a woman who looks like she just crawled out of bed and never looks at her self in a mirror.

Mr. Watson tapped his wife gently on her shoulder to get her attention. She was busy scrubbing potatoes in the sink. He motioned for the girls to come closer. "Dear," he addressed his wife, "This is Anna. She is seeking employment with us." Mrs. Watson wiped her hands on her well worn apron and turned to look in their direction. She spoke sharply and loudly, "What can ya do? Are ya used to hard work? Are ya willing to get your hands dirty?" Anna said, "Aye, I'm not afraid of work."

"We need an upstairs maid, Think you can do that?" Anna nodded her head up and down. Mrs. Watson went on "We expect you to be up before dawn, work till you're done then the rest of the day is yours but no men are to come to your room and no drinking or food eaten upstairs. We run a respectable hotel here." Mrs. Watson talked on and on. Besides cleaning guest rooms, she was to do the laundry and ironing, and mop the floors. In return for her good work habits and dutifully doing all her work, she could have three meals a day and have her own room and be paid 50 cents per week. Sunday morning she could attend church. When Mrs. Watson finished, Anna assured her she would follow all the rules.

Mrs. Watson spoke sharply to her husband. "Get them a piece of pie and some lemonade, William. You two go out to a table and he'll bring it out to ya." "I'll be here 1st of September," said Anna as she and Flora turned around and went out the swinging doors and sat at one of the tables.

Mr. Watson brought them each a generous sized piece of cherry pie and a tall glass of lemonade. "Hope you enjoy it." He said as he set it before them. My wife's a bit hard of hearing and a bit gruff when speaking but that's only because she works too hard and gets little sleep. Then he left them alone.

Flora was dying to ask Anna some things but she held her tongue. Anna was deep in thought. She felt pleased with herself. She had gotten herself some work right here at the BUFFALO HEAD HOTEL.

As they put the last bite of pie in their mouths, a clock began chiming. They both got up and carried their dishes to the kitchen. They said a hasty thank you to Mrs. Watson and were about to go through the swinging doors when a young man came falling through the doors and landed at their feet. "Seth" Mrs. Watson snapped at the young man. "Just what is the meaning of your behavior?" Picking himself up and looking from the two strange girls back to Mrs. Watson, not seeming to know what to say, he managed, "Sorry ma'ams. But, thar's a man outside a lookin' fer ya, if ya are from Boonville." Both together said, "Thanks" and went to find their kettle. Before leaving Anna scooped out a pail full of berries and hurried it back into the kitchen. "Here's some berries we picked and want you to have. Could I pour them into a basin?" Mrs. Watson reached for one under her sink. Anna poured them and said they had to hurry. John was there to take them home. Flora was trying to carry the kettle by herself when Seth picked it up away from her. Flora opened the door. John jumped down and took the kettle from Seth. He had left a space right behind his seat for it. It was raining hard. John covered the kettle with a flat board and a canvas. Then helped Anna up in the back and covered her with another canvas. Flora had climbed up on the seat and John covered them both as best he could.

Neither girl minded the soaking rain. They were both full of their own thoughts. Anna was so happy wondering what lay ahead. She settled in the wagon, warm under the dark canvas. She hummed all the songs she could think of as the horses clipped clopped back to Boonville. Flora cuddled close to John and he wrapped an extra heavy coat around them.

Chapter 8

THE WEDDING GIFT

Anna wished the days would stop slipping by so fast. She wondered if she had done the right thing. It was so hard to know what the future held. Did she really make the right decision? One moment she was sure she should write the Buffalo Head Hotel and tell them she had changed her mind and she wouldn't be there next month. Then, the next moment she was sure that she had made the right decision. On the one side she should stay here where she knew what was expected of her and everyone was kind to her, but on the other side, something inside her head kept saying that she had made the right choice. She decided she would trust God to help her.

There was one thing going on around her she knew for sure, and that was she was losing her roommate. Ever since John had proposed to her, Flora's head was stuck in the clouds. She didn't blame Flora any. It must be fun to be engaged and planning a wedding. She had to admit she was a bit envious of Flora. The wedding was to be the end of September. It wouldn't be the same here at the Hulbert House with her best friend gone, so maybe it was best to be moving on. Maybe Forestport held something, and maybe even someone, very special for her. God, what lies ahead for me? I will put my trust in you. Suddenly, she realized that she had not heard one word of the day's sermon. She hoped no one sitting around her had noticed her inattentiveness. She liked being in church. She'd have to remember to ask John if there was a Catholic Church in Forestport. She hoped so. Mrs. Watson said she would have time on Sunday to go to church.

It was hard to keep her mind from wandering. She decided she'd read the Bible this afternoon just like she did at home on Sundays. Home. She had better not think about home. She did miss Momma. She had not written about changing work places. She'd write her a long letter.

She'd also keep herself busy all afternoon. Then she wouldn't be full of self pity and homesickness. Momma used to tell her that self pity was the devil's delight and one must conquer it. The minute it was around, throw it off one's shoulders. She'd keep herself busy! She still had three borrowed books to read and other things to get done before she'd be ready to move from Boonville. The first on her list was to find a wedding gift.

Two days went by before Anna had an afternoon with some spare time all to herself. She opened her dresser drawer and reached to the back where she kept money in an old, worn-out black stocking. She counted out some of it and put the rest away, taking only what she felt she could spare. She put on her best dress and shoes. She pinned her hat on her head tucking the veil up out of the way. After putting on her gloves and picking up her purse, she went down the back stairs and around the hotel to the street. It was a warm summer afternoon. As she strolled up one street and down another, she couldn't help stopping in several of the fancy stores just to try on a hat or two and feel the material of the store made clothes. She finally reached the mercantile which had a little of everything. Anna hadn't made up her mind what she was going to buy. She took her time looking around. She looked at dishes, pots and pans, lamps and cutlery. She thought long and hard over the choices. Most everything was out of her price range. Next, she looked at the linens and cloth goods, the threads and yarns. After some time she decided to buy colored crochet thread along with a large ball of white. She carefully counted out the coins asked for by the clerk. Big Tommy had asked her to pick up some baking items for him. She was glad she had thought to bring along a basket. Anna checked them off her mental list as the clerk put in a box of cornstarch, baking powder, almond flavoring, 4 fresh lemons and a dozen eggs.

Still having some time, she crossed the street and enjoyed a leisurely walk back. At the hatters, she couldn't resist going in and asking if she might try on the light blue hat with the three small feathers that was on display in the window. She set the basket down, took off her well worn hat, and oh so carefully set the pretty new hat on her head while looking into the mirror. It felt so comfortable on her head. The sweet old lady who worked at the store told her it was so becoming on her. That no one, of all the ladies who had tried it on, did it justice like she did. That it was made for her and her alone. Anna was very taken with it until she asked how much it cost. Then, she quickly removed it and handed it back to the woman. What was she thinking? Why, she was being silly to even think she could buy such an expensive hat. She thanked the woman, put her old hat back on, picked up the basket and hurried herself back to the hotel. She was ashamed for even considering spending any of her hard earned money so frivolously. She scolded herself all the way home.

She was glad Flora was not in the kitchen when she got back. She left the basket with Big Tommy and quickly went to her room. She hid the purchases under her side of the bed.

Anna changed her dress and shoes. She took a minute to repin her hair and then headed down the stairs. She met Flora on the way. "Whar ya been? I wanted ya ta help me pick out the material for my wedding suit and go ta Mrs. Graves with it for a fittin" Flora said with a lot of disappointment. Anna told her that Big Tommy had sent her on an errand and she had spent some of the time enjoying the walk. Flora accepted Anna's answer and said she'd see Anna downstairs in a minute.

Anna and Flora served dinner and then the two of them ate. They had to do clean-up today because both Big Tommy and Caroline had taken the afternoon off. Since Flora was around, Anna couldn't start her new project. She chose to finish reading the latest book out under the maple tree. It felt good to be off her feet. She removed her shoes and stockings and sat curled up in the shade until Flora came to get her. It was time to work in the kitchen. It was Anna's turn to make the salad platters. Caroline had taught her how to make roses out of radishes, carrot curls out of thinly sliced carrots, fill celery chunks with a soft cheese, and arrange pickled beets, olives, and pickles in the center of each platter. Next she peeled and sliced cucumbers and some onions. She mixed sour cream, dill seeds, salt and pepper in a bowl and added the sliced cucumbers and onions. She set them in the icebox to chill. Next, she checked to be sure the butter dishes, the salt and pepper shakers, the sugar bowls and creamers were filled and ready for the tables. Then she sliced the loaves of fresh baked bread that Big Tommy had been making when she was off on her errands that morning. She arranged the sliced bread in cloth covered bread baskets and tucked the towel around them so they wouldn't dry out. Big Tommy had made peach cobbler for dessert. She got the sauce dishes out and extra teaspoons beside them. She checked to be sure the heavy cream had been whipped up for topping the cobbler. Big Tommy was helping Caroline with the rest of the supper. All her work was done for now so she went to see if Flora needed any help. She had used her free time picking flowers. Flora loved picking anything – flowers, berries, tomatoes, beans, even weeds. She had told Anna many stories about helping at home with the family garden. Flora loved flowers the best. She had studied and learned the names of the wild flowers. Mr. Simcourt appreciated her finding fresh flowers for the tables. Anna found Flora arranging the flowers in vases.

As Anna placed the vases around the dining room her mind went back to the whipped cream. She knew how to do it, now, but her first time didn't work out so well. Momma had made a special pumpkin pie for Poppa's birthday. He never wanted to be fussed over but his favorite dessert was pumpkin pie. Anna insisted that she knew how to whip the cream so Momma let her. Momma was busy finishing up the ironing and since Anna had said she knew how to do it, she wasn't going to ask Momma for any help. Well, Anna beat and beat and beat the cream until she had beaten it so much, it turned to a soft butter. Once it was turned to butter she couldn't change it. Lucky for her, Poppa had not come in the house yet when Momma discovered what Anna had done. Anna knew that cream was hard to come by and they rarely used any. It was sold with the milk and every penny was needed – not wasted. That night, Momma used that soft butter in the mashed potatoes and winter squash and on top of the string beans. She hid the rest down on the cellar step to be used the next day and to get it out of Poppa's sight. Poppa said how good the vegetables tasted and he didn't seem to notice that they ate pumpkin pie without any cream topping. Anna never knew if Poppa ever found out about her mistake or not but she always remembered it and was very careful never to do that again.

Flora and Anna did the dishes and pans for Big Tommy. Then John came to take Flora off somewhere. That suited Anna's plans perfectly. She could start her crocheting. It was a warm night so the window was open and Anna would be able to hear when John and Flora came driving the horse and buggy into the driveway and out behind the hotel. Anna got a good start on the surprise wedding gift. She was able to work several hours on it before she heard John's laugh. Anna put it in a pillowcase and slid it under the bed, blew out the lamp, and waited to hear Flora tell all about her drive with John.

Flora did have exciting news to tell Anna. John had asked her to go to Poland with him to meet his relatives and stay at his grandparents' house. It was a long ways from here so they would be gone for four days. Anna didn't hear anything else Flora told her that night, she was too busy planning in her mind how she would spend those four days with Flora gone.

It wasn't how Anna had planned it to go while Flora was gone. Anna had figured out the times she could work at her crocheting. But sometimes, life just isn't that simple. Other people can put a crinkle right in the middle of your plans. Anna wasn't sure if he meant to, but Big Tommy changed her plans. In fact, nothing went as Anna had planned. First of all, not only was Flora gone, but Caroline was too. That meant Anna and Big Tommy had twice the work to do in those four days. Big Tommy kept her fetching one thing after another all day. She had no free time the first day. It was well after seven that night when Anna put the last pan away. It was a nice night so she took her crocheting out to the back porch. She worked at it until she could no longer keep her eyes open.

The second day, Mr. Simcourt hired a new girl and it was left up to Anna to train her. Gerry, short for Geraldine, had never worked at a hotel or for that matter anywhere, even at home. So, Anna had to tell her every move to make. It was a long day and a total loss to

Anna as far as her project was concerned. But, she was hopeful. She still had two more days. She did sit on the back porch for an hour that second night before her eyes closed. Then she worked at it for a while laying on her bed until she woke herself up when her ball of thread fell on the floor with a thud. She decided to get some sleep. Sleep she did. Flora was not there to wake her up. She was late getting downstairs to help prepare breakfast. Big Tommy was in a temper. He banged kettles and talked to himself under his breath. Anna didn't care to hear what he was saying. She hustled as fast as she could and was grateful that Mr. Simcourt helped her with the serving. Gerry came in late. She had overslept at her house. Then, Gerry seemed to be all thumbs. She dropped silverware, she broke the handles off two sugar bowls and spilled a creamer on the kitchen floor. Big Tommy threw his hands up in the air and went out the back door letting the door slam shut behind him.

In the afternoon, Anna thought she could squeeze in an hour or two to crochet, but Big Tommy had to have several things from the mercantile. He couldn't send Gerry alone so Anna went with her. Gerry seemed to be catching on so supper serving went better. This third night, Anna decided to work in her room. It was stuffy but she was able to accomplish quite a bit before falling asleep.

She woke up on the fourth morning to a thunder storm. Big Tommy even smiled at her as she came to the kitchen. It rained hard and didn't seem to have any desire to stop. The rain brought its own set of problems. The floors were not to have mud or water on them for guests to see. That meant you kept an eye on them on rainy days and mopped often. To add to the day, Big Tommy informed Anna that he would be away from the hotel at least two hours between dinner and supper. He never was away during the day. Why today? She wanted to shout at him! He told Anna to stay in the kitchen while he was gone because he was expecting a delivery. Well, Anna thought, I will just bring my crocheting down here. She had just gotten nicely started sitting comfortably in a rocking chair she borrowed from the lobby when all of a sudden, Mr. Nichol's son, Jimmy, came bursting through the outside kitchen door dropping a bushel of green, yellow, and orange vegetables. They scattered across the freshly mopped kitchen floor. "Sorry, Ma'am" Jimmy stammered as he picked himself up hurriedly and left. Before Anna could get her hands free of the crocheting project, to set it down, Jimmy was back. This time bringing with him a gust of wind and rain, and a basket of fruits. He set the basket down on the wet floor, tipped his hat to her, and left saying something about having to get his horse out of the rain. Anna wasn't quite sure whether to cry or laugh. She set her jaw and pierced her lips tight shut and began picking up the scattered beans.

By the time Big Tommy returned to the kitchen, Anna was sitting in her chair crocheting like nothing had happened. She decided that today had more than made up for her lateness yesterday morning.

Anna really did miss Flora, especially, at meal time. They would work and talk quietly together as they got everything ready to serve. Flora was fun and easy to be around. The time passed by much faster. Gerry was quiet and very hard to get to know. Anna had not heard her laugh and she hardly smiled. But, she was trying to learn and not be so clumsy.

Big Tommy didn't talk much. When he did it was to ask for something he needed. She had never heard him carry on a conversation with any one. She really only knew what Flora had told her. She had heard that he had been a slave. He had worked along side his mother, doing kitchen work all his life. His mother had always been a slave and owned by a very cruel slave master. The slave master beat them for no reason especially when he was drunk. The drunker he was, the more lashes he gave both Big Tommy and his mother. One night when Big Tommy was around ten years old, he and his mother fled. They ran north and never looked back. His mother died some years ago. Flora heard that Big Tommy was saving his money to go to California because that's what he had promised his mother.

The rain didn't stop all that day. Anna had kept Gerry doing the mopping Anna was glad she had the bedroom to herself. It was the

49

end of the fourth day and she wanted to get as much done in the remaining time before Flora returned. Anna worked at it until she just had to stop and go to sleep. She had just put it away under the bed and was going to blow out the lamp, when Flora entered the room soaking wet. Anna helped her out of her wet clothes and handed her a towel to dry her hair.

Flora and John had had a wonderful trip, until today. The wagon of supplies John was hauling to Boonville, got mired in the mud more times than Flora cared to remember. At first it was funny, but after the third time it was just a lot of hard work. They had to get off the wagon and dig out the wheels as the horses slipped and slid and kicked mud into their faces. Somehow they made it. She was glad to be in out of the rain and lying in a dry bed.

"How were yur four days without me around? Did ya even miss me?" Flora asked. Anna blew out the light before answering so Flora wouldn't see her smiling to herself. She told Flora she did miss her and was glad she was back safely. Then she squeezed her friend's hand and they both fell soundly asleep.

It was the last Saturday of August and the annual Boonville Community dance. This was a special dance and Anna had planned to go but decided she must finish her project. It took some convincing but finally Flora and John agreed to let Anna stay home and get her packing done. The hotel was dead quiet when everyone had gone to the dance. She thought probably she and Big Tommy were the only ones in all of Boonville that were not at the dance. She had to get Flora's gift done tonight. Her mind did wonder what Big Tommy did every night alone in his room. Well, she couldn't take time to speculate on him, she must finish. After she crocheted the finishing edges all around the outside, she was done. It had taken her longer than she anticipated. She was pleased with her work. She was glad Momma had insisted she learn how to do all kinds of handiwork. It was paying off. She never could have afforded to buy anything as nice looking as this. She wrapped it in some brown paper she had seen in the kitchen and Big Tommy had let her have it. He had handed it to her without asking any questions. She had bought some gold ribbon at the mercantile and a silver sugar spoon. She tied the spoon with the ribbon on top of the gift. She slipped the gift under the bed and crawled into bed.

Today was Anna's last day in Boonville. Since it was Sunday, as usual after breakfast dishes were done and the tables set up for dinner, Anna and Flora met John at church. Anna thought it was an especially good service today. In fact, she intended to enjoy this day to its fullest and not think about leaving tomorrow.

Anna and Flora waited on customers and cleared the tables, but before they could set them for supper, Mr. Simcourt asked the girls to stop what they were doing and come into the small dining room with the fireplace. Big Tommy and Caroline were already in there. Mr. Simcourt motioned for them to sit down. At first, Mr. Simcourt said how proud he was of each of them. He spoke to Flora about her up coming wedding and how proud he was of her and how much he had appreciated the flowers she found and arranged for the tables. Then he addressed Anna. He complimented her on what a good worker she had been and how he would miss her but he wished her well.

He nodded to Caroline. She went to the kitchen and came back with a gift for Flora and one for Anna. Anna opened hers and it was a small book of prayers. Flora opened hers and found it was a wedding scrapbook. They thanked Caroline for her thoughtfulness. Big Tommy handed each of them a wooden box. It wasn't just any old box. It was one he had taken the time to smooth and paint. Each box had a hinge so it could be opened from the top. On the top of Anna's was pasted a picture of a girl reading under a tree. On top of Flora's, Big Tommy had pasted a picture of flowers in a vase. Each girl was overwhelmed with surprise. They shook Big Tommy's hand and thanked him with words and smiles. Then Mr. Simcourt handed each of them a wrapped package. Anna's contained a pretty blue apron with two big pockets. Anna had never had a store-made apron before. She thanked him and shook his hand. Flora opened her package and discovered a china teapot, sugar and creamer that all matched and had beautiful flowers painted on them. While Flora was thanking

Mr. Simcourt and reaching for her handkerchief to wipe her tears away, Anna rushed from the room. She raced up the stairs and got the gift under her bed. She had planned to give it to her later tonight, but this was a better time. She went downstairs and handed it to Flora who admired the sugar spoon on the top. Then she slowly untied the gold ribbon and opened the brown paper to reveal the special crocheted table runner. She held it up and they could all see the flowers – pink ones, yellow ones and blue ones scattered around the center with a special edging of pink, yellow and blue. Flora hugged Anna and the tears really streamed down her face as she tried to tell her thank you.

The surprises were not over yet. Mr. Simcourt ushered them all into the kitchen were Big Tommy had all the fixins to make homemade ice cream. Each of them took a turn at cranking the wooden ice cream maker. Caroline went home and brought back her two girls. They took their turn at the cranking and finally, it was hard enough to eat. Too soon it was time to get back to work. Supper had to be served and customers were already coming into the dining room. She and Flora talked long into the night. Their last night together.

Chapter 9

WHAT LIES AHEAD, AYE?

"Time we were a goin'," John said as Anna and Flora held fast to one another beside the loaded wagon. They both had to dry their tears before John helped Anna up onto the seat. He gave Flora a quick hug and swung upon the seat beside Anna. Flora had planned to go along with them to Forestport, but she was needed here at the hotel. Gerry wasn't moved in yet, taking Anna's place, and wouldn't be coming until tomorrow. Her family had had a death in the family and she had to stay with them another day. So Flora would be the only waitress working. Flora stood and waved. She watched long past their going out of sight. She would miss, Anna. She stood praying silently for good things for Anna and a safe trip for John.

"John, is there a Catholic Church in Forestport, aye?" Anna asked as they started on their way leaving the streets of Boonville behind. "Sure 'nough is. I was baptized there along with all my brothers and sisters." John answered her. He continued to almost talk an ear off Anna. He told her all about his family and everything he could think of that he knew about Forestport. The time flew by and it seemed that before one could have said 'jack rabbits' ten times in a row, the bridge over the Black River came into sight.

John stopped talking and whoaed to the horses. He put the brake on and laid the reins on the seat. He stepped down slowly to the ground, listening for something. Anna had closed her eyes and was picturing the town John had described. She was confused when she opened her eyes. She was used to him stopping every so often to rest the team. This was different. She watched John walking to the bridge. He was holding his hand over his eyes like he was scanning for something. He walked back with a quick step and motioned for her to remain quiet and to stay seated. Then almost in a whisper, he said, "I don't want to spook the horses, but somethin' sure ain't right up ahead."

"How do you know that, aye?" asked Anna in a whisper. "Cause. It's different for this time a day. Ya see that there mill pond to yer left?" Anna nodded her head 'yes'. John went on, "Thar's nobody around. Deserted. This time a day, should be lots of men workin' the logs on the river." John walked to the side of the horse closest to him and taking ahold of the harness, said "giddyup". Both horses obeyed the command. John led them across the plank board bridge speaking quietly to them all the way.

He walked the team to the General Store and unloaded the wagon. They left the horses at the livery. Then they picked up her belongings and started walking the way they had come. When they reached the General Store, John went up the steps. John said it looked like everyone had run out of town. Something definitely had to have happened. But what and where? They passed the bridge and kept walking towards the Buffalo Head Hotel. As they came around a bend in the road, there was a lot of commotion. There were people up ahead, in the road and all along the sides. People were blocking any view of what was ahead. John set his load down saying "Stay here. I'll go see what is going on. I'll be back as soon as I find out." Anna was glad to set things down and rest her arms. She hoped John would hurry and come back. Minutes passed before John returned. He was quite out of breath but able to say, "Sorry ta take so long. Some kind of train wreck. I couldn't get close enough to really see if anyone was hurt. I heard there are two train cars off the tracks. Too many people in the way. C'mon, let's work ourselves to yer hotel."

They picked up her satchels and started towards the crowd. They couldn't get through so John led her in another direction. She followed, keeping up as best she could with his long strides. They came around to the back of the hotel. The door was unlocked as they entered, Anna didn't know where it led so she kept close to John. They went through some kind of a storage room, and came to another door. John opened it. Now they were in a large kitchen. It was the one she and Flora had been in to meet Mrs. Watson.

"Who's there?"

Mrs. Watson called out as she heard someone coming into her kitchen. John let Anna step in front of him. "Just me." Anna answered. She turned and introduced John. "Glad ya made it. What a mess we got out there!" Mrs. Watson said as she nodded her head in the general direction of outdoors. Her hands were busy stirring something in a large bowl. Haven't got time to explain right now. That crowd will be comin' in here for something to eat and I aim to be ready for 'em. Can ya beat up some cream to go on top of this here gingerbread? I've got to get it a bakin"

Anna took off her hat and laid it on the things she and John had set down by the kitchen door. John asked. "Could I get a drink of water? Then, I'll be on my way." Mrs. Watson told him to help himself and thanked him for bringing Anna in the nick of time. Anna shook John's hand before he went back out the same way had they had come.

Anna found an apron hanging by the sink and put it on to cover her next-best dress, washed her hands, and asked where she'd find the cream. Mrs. Watson got the hand beater and bowl while Anna looked in the large ice box for the cream. Then she set to making lemonade. It being so hot today, Mrs. Watson reasoned they'd be needing a cool drink.

Mr. Watson stuck his head in the swinging door to see how it was going for his wife. He was surprised to see Anna. He didn't know that she had arrived. He came right over and shook her hand. He said he expected people would soon be coming for a meal. Mrs. Watson said she was ready for a herd of buffalo and to just send them in. Anna smiled to herself upon hearing that.

As soon as Mr. Watson left the room, two others came through the swinging door. Mrs. Watson introduced them as Clara and Seth. She sent Seth out for lots of ice from the ice house. The minute he was back from that, she sent him for something else. Anna couldn't help but notice how she kept Seth a hopping. Everyone was too busy to explain to her about the train wreck. She helped Clara make a mountain of meat sandwiches. Anna stayed in the kitchen with Mrs. Watson and Seth. Clara and Mr. Watson kept that swinging door a moving. They were busy waiting on people in the dining room. Hours passed before it all stopped. Just as suddenly as it had begun. Now, they could take a breather and sit down to eat.

After helping Seth and Clara with the dishes, Seth picked up Anna's satchels with her following him right up the stairs. He stopped at the far end of the long hall. He set her things inside the door and left. With the light from the hallway, she found the bed. Good, it was all made up. In the dark, Anna quickly removed her clothes, crawled into bed murmuring softly to God. "Thank you for this day, but I am glad it's over."

Chapter 10

EARLY TO BED, EARLY TO RISE, MAKES A MAN CHIPPER AND WISE

The next thing Anna knew, Seth was knocking on her door. At first she thought it must be the middle of the night but when she opened her eyes, she could see a hint of light from the window. She told Seth she'd be downstairs shortly. In the dim light, she found a dress. She would have liked it better if she could have ironed it first but since that was not possible, she pressed at the wrinkles with her hands. It would have to do. She found some combs and wound her hair up and away from her face and shoulders. She would have washed her face but she had no water.

Seth was waiting for her in the kitchen. He motioned for her to follow him. They went through the kitchen and to the door she had entered yesterday which was the storage room. It was dark in there so Seth lit the wall lamp. He showed Anna where the mops hung and where the mop pail and wringer were stored. Then he motioned for her to return to the kitchen. He had already filled the reservoir on the stove and the water was hot. He dipped the water out and into the mop pail. Then he added the washing soap. Anna could smell the strong lye in the soap. He told her to always do the dining room floor first. Then to mop the kitchen. Anna began mopping the dining room while Seth went to the kitchen. When she had finished, she carried everything back into the kitchen. Seth showed her how to remove the wringer from the pail and carry the pail of dirty mop water out through the storage room and out to where it could be dumped.

All this time, Seth had been busy filling the wood box and refilling the water reservoir. Milk and cheese had been delivered so Seth put them in the large ice box.

It had been late and everyone so tired last night that the tables were not set for breakfast. Anna dumped the last of her mop water out and put mop and pail away. She helped Seth set the tables. As they put the silverware, linen napkins, salt, pepper, sugar and butter on each table, Seth told Anna what he knew of yesterday's train wreck. It seemed it all happened because a cat ran in-between the legs of some horses. The owner of the team of horses, Mr. Breen, had stopped his horses by the train tracks. His wagon was loaded with crates of live chickens he planned to put on the train. His dog was sitting on the seat next to him. His dog hates cats and when the dog saw a cat running under the horses, he jumped off the seat to chase it. The commotion spooked the horses. They jerked forward onto the tracks right in front of the train. The train couldn't stop in time and hit the horses. The wagon tipped over throwing Mr. Breen and the crates in all directions. The horses had to be shot because they had broken legs. Some chickens got loose when the crates broke open and they had to be rounded up. Mr. Breen was carried over to Doc's house but no one knows if he will live. Doc says he has a lot of broken bones and is unconscious. It may be days before Doc knows if he will live or die. He continued to say that because the train was stopped so abruptly, two cars were derailed. Special train repairmen had to be telegraphed to come get the cars back onto the track. It will be a while before trains can come here. The broken cars are blocking the tracks.

Clara came down the stairs. "You, two, have been busy. I overslept. I'm sorry I wasn't down here to help you set the tables. Have you checked the registry yet, Anna?" Anna nodded "no". "Come with me." Anna followed Clara out the dining room and into the hotel lobby. Clara went behind the high desk, Anna followed. "Each morning you have to check the registry book to see what rooms were rented out. Write the room numbers down on paper and tuck it in your apron pocket. Then look in the cubbyholes here on the wall. If the key is in the cubbyhole, you can clean the room. Here is the master key that opens all the rooms. Pin it to your apron so you never lose it. Now, come with me and I'll show you where we keep clean bedding."

Anna followed Clara out around the desk, across the room and up the stairs. At the top of the stairs was a hallway with closed rooms on each side. Each door had a number. At the far end was a door that opened into a room with shelves lining each wall. The shelves held sheets, pillowcases, blankets, pillows, curtains, and cleaning supplies. On hooks were brooms, mops and dust mops. Using the master key, Clara opened a room she knew was vacant. She explained to Anna how each room was to be cleaned. Then she showed Anna another way to get downstairs from this linen room. At the bottom of this stairway, they entered the kitchen. Clara helped Anna set up the wooden ironing board. Seth had already started a fire in a small round stove. Clara showed Anna where the irons were kept in the storage room that had to be heated on the small stove. She left to assist Mrs. Watson with the breakfast.

Anna found a basket of tablecloths and linen napkins to iron. She kept busy ironing while Mrs. Watson was cooking breakfast. Clara and Mr. Watson waited on customers, and Seth was kept busy fetching this and that for everyone. Then, when all customers had been served, Clara came and got Anna. Now they could eat. Anna was more than ready. They each had a bowl of hot oatmeal, two fried eggs, a slice of ham, a side dish of stewed prunes, two slices of homemade bread and coffee.

Seth helped Clara with the dishes while Anna checked the registry and headed off to clean three rooms. There was more to being an upstairs maid than she had expected. She put fresh sheets and pillowcases on each bed in the three rooms, dusted the furniture, dust mopped the floors, and took the scatter rugs and the washbowl and pitcher downstairs. She went out the back door to shake the rugs. Then washed the bowl and pitcher and dried them before carrying them back to the rooms. She checked the oil supply in each wall lamp and lastly she saved the worse task until last. She had to take each chamber pot down and out to the outhouse where she dumped them. Then she had to wash them. She carried boiling hot water from the cook stove reservoir out to an old wash tub. After she left them out there to air dry, she went back and mopped the bedrooms, the hall and stairs. Then she had to wash the bedding. It was a super warm day to hang the wash. Anna enjoyed every minute of her time outside. It was fall. The trees were beginning to change color. The flocks of birds were gathering in the trees and flying overhead. So far, Anna liked it here.

After eating her dinner meal with Clara and Seth, she went back to the ironing. She had more tablecloths and some sheets to finish and put away. Then, Mrs. Watson said she was done for the day. Anna used the remainder of the daylight hours to settle her room. It was dark when they had supper and she was well ready for bed. As she and Seth walked up the stairs together Seth said, "Early to bed, early to rise, makes a man chipper and wise". She had to smile to herself as she crawled into bed. Anna liked him, even if he was a bit, not all there. She wasn't quite sure how she felt about Clara. She lay wondering why God had directed her to come here. She felt God had something special in mind for her, but what was it?

Chapter 11

STELLA

Anna settled into a routine. She knew her duties and found if she hurried on the days they had fewer guests, she had more free time to herself.

One afternoon she walked with Seth to the General Store. He got the items on Mrs. Watson's list then he showed Anna around town. He pointed out the Catholic Church and told her who lived in each house along the way. They walked past the Odd Fellows Hall where he had walked Clara and her to the last dance. Instead of walking toward the hotel, he took Anna down to the mill pond. He liked to watch the men working the logs on the Black River and sending them in to be sawed. Seth took Anna inside to watch. It was too noisy in there. She headed him back outside towards the hotel but he went up another street and showed her the town library. She was glad to know how to find it.

She was also glad to have Seth to herself. She had been wanting to ask him about a certain young man.

"Seth, who is the man that comes driving four horses and picks up men at the hotel, aye?" "Oh, that's Wes Stone. He works at the livery. He drives mostly to North Lake, I guess." Seth went on. "He came a few years ago. Only time I see him is at the hotel and at the dances. He's sweet on Stella. I try to dance with her but all the other men seem to ask her first." Seth said.

Anna just listened. Oh, she knew who Stella was. She'd seen her at the store—men always trying to get her attention and at the dances, you couldn't miss how the men flocked around her like bees to a honeycomb. Anna had to admit Stella was pretty and she wore the nicest dresses and hats. Anna had seen her type before though, beautiful on the outside but what lie beneath the surface?

Anna suggested they hurry back before Mrs. Watson boxed Seth's ears for being gone so long.

Wes Stone as a teen

Chapter 12

WES STONE

Wes Stone slouched back on the seat. They were a few miles out of Forestport, yet, so he had time to take it easy. He had full confidence in these four horses. They knew the way home and they were as anxious as him to get to the stable. It had been a long two weeks at North Lake. A couple of days or a week was the usual time, but this group of businessmen were spending their time for pleasure as well as contracting for timber. Most men came from New York City but these men were from Boston, Mass.

He relaxed his hold on the reins. The warm September breeze felt good blowing at his mustache but the sun beating on his face caused him to pull his hat down over his eyes. He let his mind wander back to the last conversation he had had with Stella. He wasn't just sure where he stood with her, his special gal. At least, that's the way he thought of her. She had talked on and on. He had just listened. One minute she said she was content to stay at home helping her parents run the General Store in Forestport. They needed her since she was their only child. Then she'd quickly change her mind and say she just couldn't stand to spend one more winter cooped up in what she called this 'country hamlet.' That she had to get away and see what was out there in other places she had read about like Cleveland, St. Louis and New Orleans. They sounded much more exciting to her than any town here in the Adirondack Mountains of New York State.

He did know a little about how she felt. After all, he had been just as restless tossing and turning night after night before making his own mind up to leave Flinton and set out for America. He had left home and Canada at age 19. He had found it hard at times— moving from one place to another finding work here and there but never really feeling settled until he came to Forestport, New York. He enjoyed driving coach from April till late October, mostly taking men to North Lake. They would get off the train at Forestport Station, spend the night at the Buffalo Head Hotel where he'd pick them up and drive them the fifteen miles to North

Lake Hotel. Then from November till mid March he'd work at the logging camp on Beaver River.

This had been his routine for a few years but now that he liked Stella, he might just settle down. After all, he liked the idea of having a wife to come home to and maybe, even having a son or two. Stella was a looker and he did enjoy being with her. But, was he ready to be married? Yes, he was. By golly that's just what he'd do soon as he had taken care of the horses.

He sat up, pushed his hat back on his head took up the reins as they approached the hotel. He left the men, and drove toward the stable. He hoped the owner, his boss, C.J. Brockstead was there. He wanted to finish work as fast as he could and go see Stella. He had to talk to her about his decision.

"George" Wes yelled out to the young boy who came running towards him. "Where's C.J.? Have ya seen him today?"

George Welch seemed to always be hanging around the stable. Kind of a pest at times, Wes thought, but when you wanted to know where someone was, just ask George. He seemed to keep track of everyone who lived in the area.

"I seen him this morning headed with 'other team and wagon that away probably goin for a load of hay, don't ya think?" George answered and pointed in another direction.

"Darn Luck!" said Wes, "just when I wanted his help."

"Could I help ya?" George said pleadingly. "Ya won't even hav ta pay me. I just can't go back to any more of that school today. I'm plumb sick of it!"

"Yeah, I guess you can help at that." Wes answered. He never cared for school himself so he understood how the boy felt.

"Now, after I get these horses to their stalls, ya can water em then give em oats and hay. Think ya can do that?"

"Course I can," George said as he ran ahead into the stable. Helping Wes Stone was lots better than being in school. He'd had enough reading and adding figures for today. He had run home for lunch with Ma and the three younger ones and he was returning to school when he heard horses coming. Besides, he needed to tell Mr. Wes the news.

"Mr. Wes? Did ya hear about the train wreck?" George asked as he worked.

Wes had hung up the harnesses and was busy rubbing down the horses. "What ya talking about boy?"

"It was sumpen. Miss Ellen even let us all out of school. Everybody in town came a running. Ya see, the way I heard it, old Mr. Breen's dog ran a chasing after something and the horses reared up a throwing Mr. Breen offen his seat clear away from his wagon that went a tippen over with chickens flying this way and that. I got to help round up all we could that were still alive. They even gave me two dead ones to take home for Ma to cook up. All of us from the school got to chase 'em so we all got a dead one or two. Well anyways, Mr. Breen's horses had to be shot. The train smashed right into them and two train cars got off the rails. It'll take days for everything to get back to where the trains are going again. Boy, it was sumpen to see!"

"What happened to Connie Breen?" Wes asked.

"Oh, he's staying at Dr. Kilborn's. He's hurt badly. I'm finished a feeding. Can I do anything else?"

"No. You best run along home."

"Oh, George, if ya see C.J. coming back here tell 'em I've gone to the General Store." Wes said as he placed the curry bush on the shelf.

Wes was anxious to see Stella but he decided he had better stop by Dr. Kilborn's along the way and check out George's story. He

65

hoped Connie wasn't hurt as badly as George had said. He owed a lot of what he knew about horses to Connie.

Wes knocked on the door. Mrs.Kilborn opened it and let him in. "I heard Connie was here. Is he?"

"Yes, Wes, come in. Might be just the medicine he needs. Doctor says he's done all he can."

Connie was asleep. He looked so much older than Wes remembered him looking last time he saw him. That was just two months ago when he went after two new horses C.J. had brought from Breen's for the stable.

Dr. Kilborn came from another room. "Hello, Wes."

"Connie, wake up. You've got company." Doc said.

"Sorry to hear about your troubles." Wes said as he got close to the bed.

Tears filled the old man's eyes. "They shot my team. Bessie and Homer. I loved those two. They were my family. Oh, I know I have other horses but I loved them the most."

"What happened? Do ya feel up to talking about it?" Wes asked him. "I've been up to North Lake and just got back. Little George was a telling me bits and pieces."

Connie told him what he remembered. He was waiting for the train so he could load his crates of chickens. All of a sudden, Snoops, his pet dog, jumped off the wagon seat and chased a cat. He hates cats he reminded Wes. Well, that spooked his horses along with the train whistle sounding off loudly all at the same time and those two horses, reared upon their hind legs and then bolted onto the tracks. I tried to hold onto the reins. Then I can't remember any more. I woke up here at doc's.
"That's enough for right now, Connie, Wes can come by again tomorrow to see you." Dr. Kilborn took hold of Wes and steered

him out of the bedroom and into the parlor. He wanted to talk to Wes alone. Doc shook his head and lowered his voice, "I'm not sure he'll make it. He took a bad fall. I've set both his legs. Oh, they'll heal and I've bandaged his ribs and shoulder but I don't know what might be broken inside of him. He needs a lot of rest. Only time will tell."

"Thanks for telling me doc," was all Wes could mutter before leaving. He was still trying to process it all when he walked up the steps to the General Store. Both Mr. and Mrs. Allen were in the store. He looked around for Stella, but only saw Mrs. Allen helping a women over in the corner and Mr. Allen surrounded by three men near the cracker barrel. He walked close to the men and could hear them discussing the train wreck. "Wes, glad you're back." Mr. Allen said as he slapped him on the back. "Did ya hear the news? What a lot of excitement we have had around here. I will say it has brought us extra business what with railroad people coming and going and everyone coming in here to find out the latest news."

The three other men all spoke to Wes, mumbled something about having to get back to work and left the store.

"What can I do for ya, Wes?" Mr. Allen asked.
"Is Stella around? I was hoping to speak to her." Wes answered.
"Oh, no, Wes, she isn't here. Stella's gone visiting her cousin, my sister's gal over near Lowville."
"When will she be back?" Wes asked.
"You know Stella, Wes. I'm not just sure when she will be. She has a mind of her own. Mrs. Allen's always a telling me I give in to her too often. Hey, she is my baby. Our only child. Thought we'd have lots more babies but guess the good Lord thinks differently." Mr. Allen answered sadly.

"Could ya tell her that I want to talk with her?"

"I'll do it Wes. I'm sure she'll be glad to see you." Wes paid for a can of pipe tobacco and a box of matches and left. He walked slower than usual-his mind swirling with it all. He thought he had

had it all worked out. He and Stella would make plans for the future. Now, she was off and who knew when she'd be back. What if she didn't come back?

Then there was Connie. Looking so gravely ill. He'd have to see if he was needed to help out at Breen's. There was only another month or so before he'd head to Beaver River for the winter.

The next few days went by fast for Wes. What with getting up before sun rise to help with the horses at Breen's then working all day with C.J. at the livery, then back to feed and water horses at Breen's. Wes wasn't sure he even knew what day it was. After dinner every day, he'd hurry to doc's and visit with Connie, letting him know all was well at his place.

Stella surprised him as he was coming out of doc's house. She came almost at a run towards him and threw her arms around him. Then she twirled herself around asking "So, how do you like it?"

He wasn't sure just what she expected him to say so he cautiously said "your dress is real nice". He remembered his two younger sisters would always twirl around whenever they had on new dresses.

"No! you goose! Not my dress—my hat! Poppa ordered it special for me—all the way from New York City. It's the latest—what do you think?" Stella demanded.

"Oh, ah. I'm not a good judge of ladies duds. They all look good to me and fine on you." Wes answered hoping that would satisfy her. "How about going for a buggy ride with me tonight? You can wear your fancy hat, if ya like."

"Tonight?" Stella shook her head. "Not tonight, Wes. Momma and I are going to Mrs. Nysners to have new dresses made. I want one to match my hat so I can wear it to the dance next week. You want me to look nice, don't you?" Before he could answer she added, "You are taking me aren't you?" as she came close and took his arm in hers and drew him along towards her home.

"Of course I am," Wes said "But I have another trip to North Lake—leaving early in the morning." "Oh, you're always going off. "Wes, what did you want to talk to me about? Poppa said you came special the other day."

"It will have to wait till I get back. Guess, we'll talk then. Stella I have to get back to the stable. But, I'll be back to pick you up for the dance." He had to get back to work. He left Stella standing in the road.

Chapter 13

EMBARRASSING MOMENT—NEVER FORGOTTEN

The fall that had been so very nice suddenly turned nasty with a cold biting wind and driving rain.

Seth was good about softly knocking on her door as he passed by on his way downstairs each morning. Maybe he had knocked, if he did, she had either not heard him or had fallen back into a deep sleep. At any rate, she overslept. What woke her was the wind driving rain beating against her window. She opened her eyes and a flash of lightning followed by a loud clap of thunder. She hurried as fast as she could to make up for her lateness. Seth tried to help. He had the mop pail full of hot water and was scraping the soap pieces into it when she reached the kitchen. Even forgetting to thank him, she began mopping the dining room and then the kitchen. She didn't take time to change the water. It was extra dirty when she finished. She hurried with it to the back door. She opened the door and heaved it. The wind was strong and the dirty water went flying in one direction and the pail flew out of her hands in another direction. At the very moment that Anna had thrown the water, Wesley Stone had suddenly come around the corner of the hotel. He was nearly drenched. He jumped out of the way saying, "What the Devil!"

That was all Anna heard. Her head had been turned in the direction that her mop pail had set sail. She turned her head toward the voice and said, "Did I get you wet, aye?"

Anna didn't hear any answer. She saw him taking long strides and disappear around the other side of the hotel. She stepped out into the rain to retrieve the pail that was rolling from side to side in the wind. She was soaking wet as she pulled herself and the pail back into the storage room and closed the door.

She leaned against the door. What just happened? Had she really just thrown water at Wes Stone? She felt so embarrassed.

She knew she could never face him. She felt like hiding in the dark room all day.

But, just then Seth came bursting into the room stumbling over his own feet.
"Oh, thar ya are! Mrs. Watson wants to talk to ya."

Anna straightened herself up. She hung up her mop and placed the pail on a shelf.

She hurried into the kitchen. Mrs. Watson was muttering to herself as she stood stirring a large kettle on the stove.

"You wanted to see me, Mrs. Watson?" Anna asked. She was sure she'd get a tongue lashing for getting the mopping done so late.

"Anna hold off your ironing today and help me. With the trains back coming and going, I hear thru the grapevine that they're full. We may have a passel of people to feed. That's what I hope. It's fall and city folks will be coming for a last hurrah before winter. We call them leaf peepers. Some will stay here while others will go north. At any rate, most will come to eat and I plan to be ready for all of them."

"What would you like me to do first?" Anna asked, grateful Mrs. Watson was in a good mood and not angry with her.

"Best you grab some bread and a bowl of oatmeal. No telling when we'll get to sit down to a meal." Then noticing Anna's wet hair and dress—"Gracious! Go change into dry clothing before you catch your death."

Mrs. Watson had heard right. Many people got off the train and hurried into the hotel out of the rain. They filled the dining room and kept Clara and Mr. Watson busy all morning. Anna worked along side Mrs. Watson dishing up breakfast foods and then started right in making dinner dishes. Just as soon as the dinner crowd was fed, supper had to be prepared, the dishes caught up and tables to be set.

Night time couldn't come soon enough for all of them. Somehow Anna was able to get Seth aside. She slipped a few cookies to him and asked him to find Wes Stone. He was to give him the cookies and say 'sorry for throwing water at him'.

That was in the morning. It wasn't until she saw Seth head for bed that she caught up to him at the top of the stairs, "Seth did you get the cookies to Wes Stone?"

"Yeah, he says to me "what ya doin' out here in the rain?" I told him Anna sends these to ya for throwing water atcha. Then I came back inside."

"But, did he say anything else?"

"No," Seth stood still and thought a minute, "Oh, something like "way to a man's heart is the stomach." "Thanks, Seth, you did well."

Anna entered her room wondering what Wes Stone might be thinking.

Chapter 14

SETH

The rain didn't let up. Anna overslept a second day in a row. She chided herself that she'd better not make it a habit, she liked working here.

When she got downstairs, Seth said he was finished with his work, could he help her with something.

"Would you check the registry to see what rooms I can clean first? We've had more people staying so it takes me longer to finish. As soon as I finish mopping down here, I'll be up but could you start taking the beds apart for me?" Anna said as she went to get the mops and pail.

Seth did check the registry and found there were two rooms' keys so he went up to them. He remembered what Anna had asked him to do – start taking the beds apart. He had never been asked to take beds apart before but he liked Anna and wanted to do what she said.

Taking the mattresses and springs off the beds was fairly easy but how do you get the frames apart? He needed a hammer. He found one in the supply room. Mr. Watson saw Seth carrying a hammer as he passed him in the hall but he assumed that Mrs. Watson had asked Seth to do something for her. He continued going downstairs to have his morning coffee.

Seth went to work hammering on a bed frame. Anna finished as quickly as she could and went to see how Seth was doing. She heard hammering. As she went up the stairs it became louder.

She found Seth bent over ready to slam the hammer on the wooden frame again. She took hold of his arm. "What are you doing, aye?" she asked in as controlled a voice as she could muster. She wasn't quite sure if she wanted to strangle him, hit him, or just yell at him. She could think of a few choice names to call him right now.

She took the hammer out of his hand. Seth couldn't understand why she was stopping him. "You told me to take the beds apart." Then she understood. She replied quietly, "Let's get these beds back together before we both get in trouble. I'll explain it to you later."

That night as she helped Clara set the tables and she knew Seth had been sent on an errand. She told Clara what had happened. They both burst out laughing.

Chapter 15

WHO IS ANNA?

Who is Anna? Or did Seth say Annie? Wesley pondered as he waited out front of the Buffalo Head Hotel for the men to climb up into the coach. He wished he'd taken a second to question Seth but Wes had just quickly tucked the package under his seat. He was in a big hurry.

As soon as the last man was seated, Wesley got the horses in motion. He was driving six instead of the usual four. With all the rain they had had lately, it would take them longer to make the fifteen mile trip to North Lake. Wesley fully intended to arrive there before night fall.

The first few miles were easy. The dirt road was hard packed with only a few mud holes. He was glad he had taken time to hitch up two extra horses for the remainder of the trip wouldn't be as easy going. He knew that from past experience. As they moved along, Wesley let his mind think about himself and Stella. He day dreamed that in the near future she would be Mrs. Stella Stone. He had fallen head over heels for her the first time he had gone into her father's general store. She had waited on him. She made him feel like he was the only person in the room when actually he recalled that there were several others shopping that day. He had even noticed that two other men tried to get her attention but she stayed focused only on him. Then the next time he saw her was at the Odd Fellows dance. It was like the two of them were magnetically drawn to each other. She had danced only with him that night and that's how it was from then on. Whenever he was in town, they went together to the dances.

But lately, she'd begun talking silly; saying such things like getting away from Forestport, going south or maybe out west. Wesley hadn't taken her seriously—just listened to her ramblings. But, last night when he took her home after the dance Stella said that she most likely would not be seeing him at the next dance—that she wouldn't be around. Before he had time to respond, she had disappeared inside her home and closed the door. He was left standing on the steps with questions swirling in his head. Now, that he had just decided to ask her to marry him and settle down in Forestport, she ups and changes completely. He wasn't sure where he stood. Did she really mean it when she talked about leaving Forestport?

The road narrowed down to just one lane. Wes had to pay attention to his driving. The usual four horses knew this road like he knew the back of his hand, but the two extra ones became skittish when the ruts were deeper and the trees thicker along both the sides of the muddy road. If his father was here right now he'd be saying "keep your mind to the grindstone, boy, or I'll box your ears when we get home".

The horses needed a rest. He stopped them close to a small stream so he could get them water. The men got out to stretch their legs. How much longer they asked as he put a grain bag over each horse's head allowing them to enjoy some oats.

"Oh, I guess, another three to four hours. Hope to get us there about dark," Wesley answered them as patiently as he could mutter. City men just didn't understand it takes lots longer to travel by horses than by train.

While the horses crunched their oats, Wesley opened the package Seth had practically thrown at him. Seth was a strange one, but likeable. Ma always said it takes all kinds of people to make the world go round. So who was Anna or did Seth say Annie? These cookies were tasty.

They reminded him of his mother. He sure missed her and her cookies. Now, why would someone named Anna or Annie want him to have cookies?

Time to get moving as he shoved the last bite into his mouth. The men were aboard so off they went. It was slower going. Deep ruts made him pay close attention so as not to tip the coach over and also to keep the horses calm.

Finally, North Lake came into view. The men cheered. In a matter of minutes they arrived at the North lake Hotel.

"Whoa" Wesley said and pulled back on the reins. All six horses stopped and Wesley locked the brake. The men got out, retrieved their baggage, and entered the hotel. Wesley drove the horses around the back to the barn. It wasn't large, like they were used to but he managed to fit all six inside.

They had worked hard for him today. As they munched on hay, he rubbed them down and spoke quietly his appreciation. After making sure each had a supply of water, he went inside the back door of the hotel. A quick bite to eat and then to bed was his plan. Mr. Cooley kept a small room behind the kitchen ready for Wesley to use whenever he brought guests.

Wes washed up in his room, combed his hair and changed into a clean shirt. Then he walked thru the kitchen to the dining room. He chose his usual corner table. Shirley, Mr. Cooley's widowed sister brought him a steaming bowl of hot stew and plate of biscuits. She left and came back with a bowl of maple syrup and large mug of coffee. She liked Wes and was about to visit with him when Marcellus came to the table. She left the two men alone.

"Hello there, Stone", Wes looked up. "Hello, yourself. What brings you to North Lake?" Wes replied. "Oh, been helping out Charles Cooley as his handyman until time to head back to Beaver River." Marcellus answered, "Mind if I sit a spell?" "Not at all, glad to have your company," Wesley answered.

"When you've finished eating, how about sharing a bottle with me? I know you drink. I saw you at camp last year, remember?"

"Shirley, bring Stone and me a bottle of whiskey", Marcellus demanded of the woman when she came to take away the empty dishes. "Add it to my bill."

Shirley came back with 2 glasses and a full bottle. Marcellus opened the bottle and filled the glasses. They downed them and Marcellus refilled them but this time, they drank the second a bit slower. They sat reminiscing about last year's logging at Beaver River. Marcellus kept the glasses refilled. Wesley caught himself falling asleep at the table. Interrupting Marcellus' telling his life story, Wesley stood and announced he was going to bed. He walked a bit unsteady and was asleep as soon as he crawled under the blankets on the narrow cot.

"Oh, my head" Wesley muttered as he swung his feet onto the floor and stood up. Then, he remembered he'd had had quite a bit to drink last night. He put on an overcoat and headed out to care for the horses. They came first. He had to be sure they did or he'd be out of a job in a hurry.

Since the men didn't finish their business they all spent another night. Wesley had spent the day in the barn. He checked over the harnesses, greased the carriage wheels, checked the undercarriage, made sure the horse feed and water supply were ample.

It was dark when he came in for his supper. Shirley served up chicken and biscuits swimming in greasy gravy but it tasted good to Wesley. There was even a large piece of apple pie for dessert. Marcellus was still hanging around so they rounded up a couple other men and played cards. The whiskey was flowing but Wesley took care to drink a bit less. He liked to drink, that was a fact but he liked to remember it the next day and not get socked with any hangover.

They all stayed another couple of days. It didn't matter to Wesley. He was paid to bring men here to contract for lumber needed in New York City. Mr. Cooley saw to it that he got meals and a bed and the Forestport livery paid for stabling, feeding of the horses and Wesley's driving.

Wesley never minded if he was in North Lake two days or a week just as long as he got to be with Stella at the next dance in Forestport. At least it had been that way for quite a spell.

Wesley thought Stella was happy with the way things were going. It ate at him. He hadn't thought of it being any different, but now he wasn't sure. Again, he wondered, did she really mean to leave Forestport?

Chapter 16

THE DANCE

Finally by Saturday the sun came out. It had rained every day for a week. Anna had had her fill of mopping floors. She had also learned her lesson when it came to throwing out the water. First, look and take a second to listen before heaving it out the back door. She did smile to herself whenever she thought about how she had nearly drenched Wesley Stone.

She hadn't meant to throw water at him and she did want to apologize for it happening. She wasn't sure if she'd be seeing him again or when she did would he be holding a grudge.

Saturday night came. As soon as the last pan was put away, Seth, Anna, and Clara changed their clothes and walked together to the dance. When they arrived, Anna saw Wesley dancing with Stella. She hoped for a chance to tell him she was sorry.

The musicians called a "Change Partner Dance". That was while you were dancing whenever the caller yelled out "change partner" everyone quickly found another person to dance with.

She was on the floor enjoying the various partners swinging her around when it happened quite unexpectedly, "Change partners" was called. Anna found herself almost flung into the arms of Wesley Stone. It happened so quickly. She had to speak fast before he went on to another.

She asked "Did I get you wet, aye, the other day, outside the hotel?"

Her question caught Wesley by surprise. He had been concentrating on the dance steps. He looked at her, this dark haired brown eyed girl in his arms.

When he didn't answer right away, Anna thought perhaps he hadn't heard her but then he said "So you're the one giving me a bath and there I was wetter than I already cared to be."

Anna managed to say "I'm sorry, aye. I should have looked before I tossed it." "What's your name?" he asked just as the caller yelled "change partners".

"Anna Burns" she said as another partner grabbed her hand and spun her in another direction and out of Wesley's sight. It was Seth. Anna hoped Wesley had heard her.

During the musicians' break time, Wesley corralled Seth before he could head for some lemonade. Wes took him by the sleeve "Seth, come outside with me. I need to ask you some questions."

Seth went with him but pulled his arm free. "What you want, Wes?" Seth asked, "I need to get something to drink."

"I've got some drink—over here in the carriage." Seth followed Wes. Wes reached inside the carriage and bought out a jug. He took off the top and handed it to Seth. "Here, take a swig."

"I'd better not. Mrs. Watson finds out she'll box my ears or worse."

"Oh, come on. Just have a quick one to quench your thirst. I need to ask you a couple of things and then you can go get your lemonade."

Seth took a swallow and choked on its taste.

"How can you drink that stuff?"

"Never mind me. I want to know about those cookies you gave me last week."

"Mrs. Watson makes em, aren't they good?"

"They were good but what I want to know is why did she give me cookies? She's never given me anything before."

"No" Seth said. "The cookies were from Anna. She said she was sorry for throwing water. Are you mad at her or something? I like Anna. She is good to me. I know she doesn't like to throw water on anyone. Are you mad?"

"No," answered Wes. "You can go back in now."

Chapter 17

CURIOSITY

Anna tried not to think about Wesley Stone. Whenever she caught herself day dreaming about seeing him again, she reprimanded herself. After all, he was smitten with that Stella Allen. Her parents owned the General Store. Every time Anna had seen Stella she was wearing a different store bought dress and a matching hat. Anna knew she shouldn't be harboring such unkind thoughts about someone she really did not know but it irked Anna that Stella seemed to have everything a girl could ever want, even the most handsome man Anna had laid eyes on.

Anna missed her friend Flora. If Flora was here Anna could talk all this over with her. Anna wished she could talk to Clara in the same way but she knew Clara would just shrug her shoulders and walk away. Oh well, if she knew what was good for her, she'd forget all about Wesley Stone. He had no eyes for her and she'd better face up to it.

Still, she couldn't forget him as she ironed the last tablecloth. Come to think of it, she hadn't seen Wesley in several days. She could ask Clara if she had seen him but then she came up with another way of finding out about Wesley. Instead of asking Seth to mail her letter to Momma, she'd walk to the General Store herself. She hoped Stella was there minding the store. Anna had heard that Stella's mother was ailing and had taken to her bed.

After eating dinner and helping with the dishes, Anna went to her room and changed into her next to best dress. She changed her shoes, put on her hat and a pair of gloves. She got the envelope addressed to Momma and found enough to buy a stamp and headed for the store. Seth had been to the store already for Mrs. Watson so Anna didn't bother to ask if anything was needed.

The day was warm and usually Anna would just walk leisurely along enjoying what was left of a nice fall day. But she felt the urgency to see Stella Allen. Anna was in luck. Stella was minding the store and she was alone. Anna noticed Stella had her back to the door and was busy dusting and rearranging some fancy glassware. Anna pretended to be interested in the yard goods and then she moved to the glassed in cabinet holding all colors of thread. It was there that Stella spotted her.

"Can I help you find anything in particular?" Stella asked.

"No. I just enjoy admiring the many colors of thread there are these days" Anna answered. She felt it was a dumb answer but she had to say something. Then Anna remarked about how nice the weather was today and on her way here she had seen a flock of geese heading south. Stella didn't say anything, just nodded her agreement.

Anna walked over closer to Stella asking as she walked, "I heard your Momma is ailing. How is she doing?" Stella said her mother had taken to her bed many times as long as Stella could remember but thanked Anna for asking.

Anna held out her letter. "I came to mail this out to my Momma in Canada." Stella went to get a stamp while Anna counted out her coins on the counter. Stella handed the stamp for Anna to lick and place on the envelope. "Wesley Stone is from Canada. Did you know that?" Stella asked Anna. Anna's eyes shot up and straight into Stella's. Anna didn't know that and she wasn't about to let Stella know how much finding that out about Wesley meant to her. Anna just nodded her head no.

"Yes", Stella went on "but I have no idea just where. We never talk about it and I guess I won't be finding out now".

Anna wondered what Stella meant by saying not now but she thought it best not to act interested in him so she said instead, "I must get back to the hotel. See you at the next dance?" Stella responded, "I've never missed one yet".

Anna walked home slowly pondering just what did Stella mean by "not now". Had Wesley returned to Canada? Anna hoped not.

Chapter 18

THE LETTER

Wesley didn't show up at the next dance, or the one after that. In fact, he wasn't at any more of them. Stella, on the other hand, never missed one. As soon as the music started, Stella as out there. She seemed to be really enjoying herself. Anna wanted to ask about Wesley, but then thought better of it. She would be content to watch and listen. But Anna heard and saw nothing of Wesley.

Winter settled in and Forestport became a very quiet town. All trains had stopped coming for weeks now and the hotel business was almost down to zero. Clara went to live with her cousin just outside of Forestport. She said she'd be back in the spring when the trains were again stopping at the Forestport Station.

Anna was glad for the library. She went each week to take out another book. She was also glad she knew how to do handiwork. She was busy making Christmas gifts. She had more time to write to everyone. They wrote back. Seth said Anna got more mail than anyone he had ever known.

Christmas came and went and the New Year, 1897, arrived with an ice storm. Later, one snow storm after another blanketed them. Anna thought about all she had seen and places she had worked since she left her home in Canada almost a year ago. The days seemed to pass slowly. Anna wondered if maybe she should go back home. It would be so great to see Momma, Pete and Maggie. She had gotten letters from them but it just wasn't the same as being with them. She counted the money in her old black stocking. She was sure she had enough to travel to Canada and enough to return to Forestport, if she wanted.

She heard someone running down the hall towards her room. She knew it had to be Seth. Before she could reach the handle of her door, Seth was calling out her name. He was about to pound on her door when she opened it. He was all out of breath and stuck a white envelope in her face.

"Look", Seth said as he tried to catch his breath. "This is from someone else, right?" Anna took the envelope and understood what Seth was saying. The postmark was from somewhere else. She turned it over to see if maybe the person who sent it had put a return address on the back but it was blank.

"Thank you" she said automatically to Seth and then she closed the door, leaving Seth standing there. Seth stood quietly outside Anna's room hoping he'd hear her say something so he'd know who wrote her that letter. He was about to knock on her door and ask her when he heard Mrs. Watson's voice calling for him. He knew from past experiences not to let Mrs. Watson wait for him. He had gotten his ears boxed many times for what she called lollygagging instead of finding out what she wanted. He took off running again.

Anna sat down on the edge of her bed and studied the envelope. She didn't recognize the handwriting or the postmark. Then she decided that it must be from her brother, Simon Burns, who was working somewhere near Carthage, NY.

Anna held onto the envelope with her left hand while she pulled a hairpin out of her hair. Using the hairpin like a pair scissors, she opened it along the top. She found a single piece of paper folded inside.

January 1, 1897

Dear Annie

I'm working in Beaver River. Don't tell Stella I wrote to you.

Wes

Anna read it over again and then held it up against her chest. She was full of emotions. Soon tears began slipping out from the sides of her eyes and trickling down her cheeks. She held fast to the letter as she was flooded with thoughts. So, Wesley Stone, who apparently wants her to remember him as Wes did think about her. He had written Annie. Maybe that's what he thought she had said her name was. No one had ever called her that before but she liked knowing that Wes thought of her as Annie.

Then, she thought, he is around; he didn't go back to Canada but is working in Beaver River, wherever that was. It doesn't matter where it is thought Anna. It must be closer than Canada. Her head raced on. He will be coming back to Forestport. She would see him again. But what about Stella? Anna sat to thinking about Stella and how she had said "not now" when Seth came to get her. Mrs. Watson wanted her immediately in the kitchen.

Anna put the envelope and letter under her pillow and hurried downstairs. She found the kitchen a flurry of activity. Seth seemed to be wandering in many directions and not sure just which way to go first. When Mrs. Watson spotted Anna she told her that she would be leaving for Remsen as soon as possible. She had decided to visit her sister and family. Since it was such a nice day, she wanted to leave and be able to get there by dark. Mr. Watson was at the livery stable arranging for a carriage. She wanted Anna to pack up some jars of preserves and peaches and wrap up a nice sized roast to take with her. Then, she left the kitchen to see about her packing.

Anna got busy. She found a wooden basket used for picnics in the storage room way up on the highest shelf and was trying to reach it when Seth came to her rescue. He was taller and able to catch hold of it and pull it down. Anna lined it with a heavy tablecloth and put in the sandwiches and added some sugar cookies from the cookie tin. Next, she filled a pint mason jar with water and screwed the metal cover on tight. That would have to do for a drink.

She gathered several jars of canned goods and a large roast from the cold cellar where the meats were stored in barrels. She was wondering just what to put them in when Mr. Watson came into the kitchen. His wife had sent him to check on her after he had gotten back with the horse and carriage. He found a small barrel and helped Anna pack everything. He sent Seth to get some heavy wool blankets.

Anna watched as Mr. Watson helped his wife into the carriage. He wrapped her legs and feet with a blanket. He set the barrel of food beside her on the seat. He wrapped another blanket around it.

Mr. Watson asked Anna if she minded getting a simple dinner for Seth, himself and her, and would she come up with something for supper later that day. Anna got busy in the kitchen. She was glad to be of help to Mr. Watson. He was such a nice man.

The next morning Seth was up before anyone. After checking on the supply of wood and getting the fires a going in the stoves he filled the water kettles. Since he had finished his usual tasks and Mrs. Watson wasn't there, he decided he would surprise Mr. Watson and Anna by fixing breakfast. He had watched Mrs. Watson make the oatmeal plenty of mornings. He did just as he had always seen her do. The problem was he made way too much for only three people to eat. Luckily Anna got down to the kitchen before he began cooking any eggs or ham.

The kindly Mr. Watson thanked Seth for his thoughtfulness but made it explicitly clear to him that from now on he was not to do the cooking

While they ate their generous helping of oatmeal, Anna asked if she might be allowed to do some baking, just while Mrs. Watson was away. Mr. Watson consented and told Seth he could assist Anna if she wanted his help.

Right after breakfast Anna set Seth to washing up the dishes while she mixed up bread dough and set it to rising. Next, she stirred up a white layer cake. Later in the day after the cake was cool she made a lemon filling and put a coconut frosting on top. She allowed Seth to stir as she measured and added the ingredients.

That evening as they sat down to supper Mr. Watson was impressed with Anna's freshly baked bread, her baked pork roast, potatoes and gravy, stewed tomatoes and her white cake for dessert. He complimented Anna on her baking skills and told her someday she would be making some young man a wonderful wife. He also added that she was on her way to becoming a great cook like his wife. Then he added something Anna had never heard before – "the way to a man's heart is through his stomach". He gave her permission to take over the kitchen while Mrs. Watson was away. He'd be sure to tell Mrs. Watson what a fine cook she was.

After supper Seth challenged Anna to a game of checkers. He won the first game and felt really proud of himself boasting to Mr. Watson about it. But after Anna won the next two games, he became sullen and headed for his room. He didn't ask Anna to play checkers again. That suited Anna just fine. She spent evenings doing what she liked doing best – reading. She did wish she could write to Wes, but she had no idea where to send it. She'd have to be content knowing he knew her name and had written to her.

Chapter 19

NEWS

What had she been thinking going back home to Canada? Of course she wouldn't be doing that! Not now! She had to be here at the Buffalo Head Hotel whenever Wes showed up. She had read his letter over and over and even slept with it under her pillow. He had written to her! She hoped that he missed her as much as she missed seeing him. Many nights now she had fallen asleep dreaming that they were out dancing, twirling together on the dance floor with everyone watching, especially Stella.

Yes, this New Year was starting out to be a hopeful one for Anna. But winter seemed to be taking it's time getting over. The days seemed long to her. She was anxious for spring. She had so enjoyed her seventeenth birthday. Mrs. Watson surprised Anna with a special spice cake all covered with that fluffy white boiled frosting that Anna loved so much.

Anna had wondered why Seth asked Mrs. Watson if he could be the one to get it from the kitchen after they had finished a delicious supper of stuffed pork chops, mashed potatoes, creamed onions and an assortment of pickled vegetables. Anna noticed Mrs. Watson nodding her consent but adding you be mighty careful ya hear! when Seth went into the kitchen. He came back through the swinging doors carrying the most gorgeous layer cake Anna had ever seen. Seth set it down right in front of Anna and then they started singing Happy Birthday to her. She fought back tears and thanked each one around the table. That was all she could get out. This was her first birthday away from Momma and she truly missed her. But she was glad she had come to America.

Spring did come. The snows melted off the tracks and the trains were back on their regular schedules. Clara had moved back to the hotel resuming her duties as waitress and assistant cook. Anna was again kept busy with the mopping, washing and ironing. It was so good to hang the wash outdoors—to smell the fresh air and see the birds busy making nests in the trees and singing their special songs. Mrs. Watson had agreed to let Anna help with the baking, but after all her other work was done. Anna's days were very busy. Anna was happy.

Anna did have one concern. What was Stella up to these days? She had asked Seth who waited on him when he went to the store and he told her Mrs. Allen. When she questioned him about Stella he just shook his head and said he hadn't seen her in a spell.

Anna had to find out for herself. She needed to find out if Stella was waiting for Wesley Stone to come back. Anna came up with a plan—Seth had gone along with Mr. Watson to get a supply of wood. They would be gone a couple of days. Anna hurried with her work and when Mrs. Watson didn't need her help in the kitchen, she asked if there were things needed at the store that she'd be willing to get them since she had a book to return to the library. Mrs. Watson made up a list. It didn't take Anna long to change her dress and shoes, put on her hat and be off with the book in one hand and a basket in the other.

First, she left the book at the library and much to old Mr. Struth's surprise she didn't sign out another book. She just gave him the excuse that she was too busy these days to read.

Anna hurried into the General Store. As she entered the door there were several people lined up waiting for Mrs. Allen. Anna decided to go around back and see if John was by any chance delivering today. She found John lifting the last bag out of his wagon. She waited until he and Mr. Allen finished with their business and Mr. Allen had gone back into the store.

John spotted her waiting to speak to him, "Hello there stranger," he said. "Haven't seen you in many months".

Anna reached out and shook John's hand. "How is Flora? I sure miss her to talk to. How is little Johnny, aye?"

"Hold on, I can only answer one question at a time," John said. Then he proceeded to tell her that Flora missed her too and that she was keeping busy what with running the house and helping him where she could with the farm work, especially when he was gone on delivery days. Baby Johnny was taking up the rest of her time and they were planning a large garden as well. In fact, he was taking home some special garden seeds that Mr. Allen carried from Utica which they didn't have in Boonville. Before Anna got to tell her news about a special beau in her life, John was up on his wagon seat and slapping the backs of the horses to get going; said he had to make tracks fast to get home before Flora sent a search party out looking for him. He'd tell Flora he saw her.

Anna walked around the corner of the store and up the two steps. There was one person ahead of her, and Mr. Allen was busy helping another man in the back corner trying on hats.

When it was her turn, Anna was glad to have Mrs. Allen. She felt a bit more comfortable asking her about her daughter. She read the list of items to Mrs. Allen. Anna waited for Mrs. Allen to add it up and put it on the hotel account. It was then that Anna asked about Stella. Anna could see by the shine in Mrs. Allen's eyes that she was pleased to talk about Stella, her only child, but as she talked Anna saw tears well up in the lady's eyes.

Anna walked home carrying the basket. She tried to remember everything that Mrs. Allen had said. Mrs. Allen had talked on and on about her Stella. What was important to Anna was what Mrs. Allen had said about Stella's leaving.

Mrs. Allen told Anna that she couldn't stop Stella from leaving, no matter what she tried to say to convince her to stay. Stella had made up her mind. She wasn't happy in Forestport anymore; she had outgrown it. That she wanted to see more of the world and had no intention of getting stuck living here. Both Mr. and Mrs. Allen tried to talk her out of it. Stella had packed up everything she owned and gone on the first train out of the Forestport Station. She had gone west. They had had a letter from Buffalo, then Cleveland, and the last letter she said was headed for St. Louis and maybe onto California. Anna had left after hearing that because poor Mrs. Allen was wiping the tears as they were starting to flow down her face.

The walk back to the hotel seemed suddenly shorter than usual. Maybe it was because Anna felt like a weight had been lifted off her shoulders and she could almost float on air. So Stella Allen was gone. Gone for good aye? Well good riddance, as far as Anna was concerned. Did Wesley know? Is that why he wrote to her, because he knew Stella's plans for leaving? Well whatever. It didn't matter, he had WRITTEN to Annie Burns. She'd be waiting for him no matter how long it took. If she didn't have this heavy basket to carry, she would have skipped all the way back to the hotel and not cared who saw her acting like a little girl.

Chapter 20

SURPRISE

April days were getting warmer and all the snow was melted. Business at the hotel was picking up. Everyone was kept busy from before sunup to way after sundown. Anna couldn't help but laugh at the way Seth would turn in circles trying hard to keep up with all the demands on him to fetch this or go there. Mrs. Watson sure depended on his agility even if he was somewhat lacking in ability.

The hotel had been busy renting out more rooms and so Anna had piles of wash to do. She got up earlier than usual to start the washing and hang them out to dry. There was only so much space on the lines. She was concentrating on hanging the sheet she had in her hands being sure it hung straight and to make it easier to iron. She had just put the final clothes pin on it when suddenly something poked the wet sheet towards her face. She jumped backwards with a fright. What could have caused it to do that she wondered and then she spied a pair of blue eyes and a black mustache. She recognized the face of Wesley Stone poking his head around the corner of the sheet.

"Wes" was all she managed to get out as he came around the end of the line of clothes.

"Now there! I've paid ya back. One surprise for another", he quipped with a silly kind of grin on his face. Before she could collect her thoughts he continued "Are you going to the dance Saturday night?"

Without any hesitation she bobbed her head up and down and squeaked out a quiet but definite "Aye". Then just as quickly as he had come he was out of her sight. Before picking up another sheet to hang she pinched herself on the arm just to make sure she wasn't having a dream and that she was awake standing outside hanging sheets and Wes had come by to ask if she'd be at the dance.

Chapter 21

WHAT WAS HE THINKING?

Why did he do that? What made him ask her if she'd be at the dance? He wasn't even sure that he'd go. As soon as he had gotten back, taken care of the horses he had practically run to the General Store to see Stella. But, it was like a horse ran over him when Mr. Allen told him Stella was gone—gone for good! The last they had heard she was on a train to California and had no plans to come home ever again.

Now, he had asked Annie to meet him at the dance. He wasn't in any hurry to get tangled up with another female—not yet and maybe never. Women were fickle. Just when you think you have life planned out, they upset the whole caboose. From now on he was going to be careful around women.

But something drew him to this brown haired, brown eyed gal from Canada. He said he'd see her at the dance so he would keep his word and go, but he'd only dance once or twice with her and that'd be it.

At least he'd paid her back by surprising her. She seemed so glad to see him. Her face did light up like a candle.

Chapter 22

WHERE DO I STAND?

Seth, Clara and Anna arrived at the dance after most others. Mrs. Watson was a stickler for everything being done before letting them go. Anna quickly scanned the room to see if Wesley was there already. The music started and Seth took her hand and led her out onto the floor. She hoped Wes would come and cut in. Seth was a good dance partner but she wanted to be in the arms of Wesley Stone. She had a few more dances with others before he did cut in. She couldn't help but notice how handsome he was. She liked his black hair and that mustache of his he curled upwards. She loved to feel his arms around her. He was something. She hoped the music would go on and on. But it did stop. He took her over to where Clara and Seth were standing and he left. She didn't see him again.

Chapter 23

MORE QUESTIONS THAN ANSWERS

Spring ended and summer was in full swing. Mrs. Watson didn't have a garden but she bought bushels of produce as it became available. Anna, Clara and Seth were plenty busy doing their usual work and helping with the canning.

Anna continued to walk with Seth and Clara to the dances. When Wes was home he'd come to the dance. He did dance with her but then he'd leave before the dance was over. Anna tried not to let it bother her, but she wondered if he would ever ask to walk her home. She didn't lack for partners. In fact, R.T. Adamson seemed to be quite smitten with her. She enjoyed spending the intermission time visiting with him. He was big and burly. Reminded her of John in Lyons Falls. He wasn't half as nice looking as Wes but R.T. made her laugh.

In late August they were all at the dance as usual. She hadn't seen Wes anywhere around so she figured he was not back from North Lake. She and R.T. had finished dancing and he had just asked if she'd like to sit down. He'd go get them something to drink when suddenly, she saw Wes come towards them. Without a word to her, Wes slapped R.T. on the back and said he'd meet him outside.

Anna didn't care to stand there alone so she walked over and asked Clara if she could be of any help making sandwiches. She kept looking towards the door wondering what made Wes act so mad?

She never saw the two of them again that night. Seth told her on the way home that Wes almost caused a fist fight with R.T. He didn't hear what it was about, but he saw Bill Boylan and Rex Johns step between Wes and R.T. and send them away from each other. They must have been told not to return to the dance.

Chapter 24

PONDERING HIS LIFE

Wes walked back to the boarding house. He wished he could have settled it with R.T.

He had asked him, "Just what are you doing R.T., with Annie?"

R.T. had stammered he didn't know that anyone had a claim on her. He hadn't seen Wes at the dance tonight, or at the last dance either, so what was he so huffy about?

Before anything more was said Bill and Rex had taken a hold of each of them, told them to go home in opposite directions and not return to the dance.

Wes slammed the door and stomped up to his room. He didn't even care if Mrs. Caldwell heard him. Mrs. Caldwell came out of her room and hobbled down to Wes's. She knocked and asked "what's wrong Wes. Anything I can get ya?"

"No, Mrs. Caldwell," Wes answered. "Just having a real bad day. Sorry I woke ya."

"Well you go to bed." She said, get a good night's sleep. Things always look better in the morning. I'll fix you a nice breakfast."

Wes laid in bed. He wasn't sleepy. The day had all gone wrong. They had gotten a late start leaving North Lake. Then half way home, Buckwheat, his lead driving horse threw a shoe. He had no way of shoeing her, so when the road widened he took hold of her bridle and walked with her. That seemed to keep all four of them calm. But, it was a hot, dusty walk and so much slower. The flies were everywhere. Everyone was out of sorts. The men in the coach complained of the slowness and the heat. Well, he was doing the best he could.

By the time he was rid of the men and gotten three other horses cared for, he walked Buckwheat to the blacksmith. She was plumb worn out. He felt sorry for her.

He still had to go to Breen's. Connie was home but not able to do much. He had little George feeding the horses but they needed exercise and brushing. George meant well but he was a bit short to do what Wes considered a good job. By the time he'd washed and put his clean clothes on, it was late into the evening. He had hoped to dance every dance with Annie tonight. But, then, when he finally gets to the dance, he sees her with R.T.

He shouldn't have lost his temper. After all, R.T. was right. He hadn't been around tonight, or at the last dance. He really didn't have any claim on her. Well, nothing could be done about it now. He'd think about it, but he needed a few hours of sleep first.

He'd have to apologize to R.T. He was a good man. Maybe Annie was sweet on him. It just doesn't pay to get mixed up with women. He fell asleep thinking—Am I getting over Stella? I do like Annie. But does she like me, especially after tonight?

September arrived. Wes no more than got back from North Lake, when C.J. had him lined up with traveling—here and there and then back to North Lake.

Connie Breen was getting along better but Wes still wanted to do his share of helping him. That left only sleep, so no time to socialize. Besides, he had sworn off women.

He was away and missed the September dances but was home by late October. He was just in time for the special Fall Frolic dance. It was a real special time for those who were "sparking". Last year he and Stella had really enjoyed it. He thought Stella is gone but Annie is here—would she care to go with him?

It was Wednesday and the dance was Saturday. He decided he could stop by the hotel to see Annie on his way to Breen's.

It was suppertime and the hotel was busy. He entered the lobby and was met by Mr. Watson.

"No one here has asked to be picked up tonight, Wes," Mr. Watson said assuming that was why Wes had stopped in.

"I was hoping I could speak to Annie Burns?" Wes asked.

"Oh, sure you can. I'll send Seth to find her. Sit down over there, Wes. I'll go find Seth". Mr. Watson left.

Wes felt a bit out of place. He decided he best not sit down on the plush chairs since he was wearing dirty work clothes. He stayed near the door. What was taking so long? Maybe this wasn't such a good idea. He was about to leave when he saw her.

Anna Burns came rushing into the room. She had an apron covering her faded dress and her hair was pinned away from her face. "Is something wrong Wes?" she asked as she came closer. "No," he answered. "Just hoped you might go to the Fall Frolic with me Saturday."

Her face lit up. "Aye. I'd like that".

'I'll be by to get ya." Wes answered. Then he turned around, grabbed the door handle and out he went. Wes whistled as he briskly walked to Breen's.

Chapter 25

FALL FROLIC

Seth and Clara had gone ahead to the dance. Anna waited up in her room. Mr. Watson told her to get ready but stay there and when Wes came for her, he'd let her know. Anna put on her Sunday dress and shoes. She spent extra time fixing her hair. Then she sat on her bed and waited.

Was Wes really going to come for her? It seemed like forever waiting. Finally, Mr. Watson knocked on her door. He took her arm and escorted her down to where Wes was standing inside the front door.

"Here she is," Mr. Watson stated as he handed her arm over toward Wes.

Wes took her hand and they went out to the carriage that C.J. let him use. Wes helped her up onto the seat then climbed up beside her.
"What's your horse's name, Wes?" Anna asked.

"Buckwheat," Wes answered.

For some reason neither of them spoke. Wes stopped next to other carriages that were lined up. He got down and tethered the horse. Then helped Anna down and into the dance hall. She danced with only Wes all evening. R.T. was there but he didn't try to cut in.

They had a wonderful time. Anna hoped the night would never end.

Chapter 26

GOING AWAY

Spring had turned into summer and then came fall. Anna was enjoying all life could offer. She was spending more time than just Saturday nights with Wesley. Whenever he was in town, he took her for long walks, usually along the banks of the Black River that flowed near by Forestport.

He told her about his work. He drove businessmen mostly up to North Lake. After breakfast on Monday he would pick them up at the Buffalo Head Hotel. It would take most all day to travel the fifteen miles up there where they would stay at the hotel. The men would contract for lumber and he would bring them back on Wednesday. The men were from large cities downstate traveling by train and usually staying at the Buffalo Head. Sometimes their wives would come along and then they would stay a week or more in one of the small cabins at North Lake.

Wesley used four horses to pull the coach, but if it was rainy and the roads were full of ruts, he took a couple of others to help pull. He had to carry spare wheels, cans of axle grease, an axe and shovel to be prepared for downed trees in the road, and be ready for any breakdowns they might have along the way.

Anna liked dancing but she did treasure their walks on Wednesday night. That's when Wesley did most of his talking. Since they had both grown up in Canada, and both came from small hamlets they had that in common. Wesley would tell her about his brother and three sisters and about his momma and pa. She did notice they had one difference. She had been brought up attending a Catholic church and Wes a Methodist.

One fall day as she sat on the back stoop scrubbing carrots for Mrs. Watson, Wesley came up to her. Since she seemed a bit startled, he thought he better explain himself.

"Thar ya are" he began. "Saw Seth out front and he said I might find you out here."

Anna straightened up her back from her bending over position and looked up at Wes, feeling a bit off balance to have him finding her like this. He never came in the afternoon and she wondered why he had suddenly shown up.

He continued "I'm off to Beaver River. Told the foreman I'd get my tail back up there as soon as I was done at the livery. Well, trains will be stopping soon".

Anna sat looking up at him trying hard to comprehend what he was trying to say to her. This was the first she heard about him going north. In fact, it had not even crossed her mind that he would be gone this winter. She stammered "But what about the horses at the livery?" She knew he cared deeply how they were cared for.

"Oh well, they will get along without me. A young boy named George has been hired to look out for them while I am gone".

Then before she could think of saying something else to try and persuade him to stay here in Forestport, he continued "I'll be back in the spring. I gave my word and I intend to keep it".

Anna stood up still trying to say something to stop him but instead she was quiet. He stepped closer holding her to him and giving her a kiss on the lips. He said softly "I want to remember this. I will be back". He released her and walked quickly around the building.

Anna stood there looking off into space and then sat back down. Those carrots got scrubbed so hard they fairly shone as tears rolled down her face. She was sure she could have filled a bucket with all of them and save Seth the trouble of carrying it so far from the pump. She finally got a hold of herself and remembered his last words—"I'll be back".

Chapter 27

1898

Somehow the days did pass one after another. A new year came 1898. For her eighteenth birthday, the Watson's saw to it that she had a special cake and some presents—some stationary, ink and pens, a box of envelopes, a new black purse, and a pair of gloves. Seth proudly handed her several letters that had come for her the last few weeks. Mrs. Watson had not let Seth walk to the store until the weather got nicer. They had had one big snow storm after another until now.

Anna was grateful for her mail but there wasn't one from Wesley. She'd have to be content with last year's letter. She knew it by heart and she kept it under her pillow. She had asked Mrs. Watson for a piece of paper off the meat wrapping roll and she made herself a calendar. As she marked off a day each night, it made her feel one day closer to seeing Wesley. She had no doubt about him. He said he'd be back and he was a man of his word.

The trains had been back running their regular schedule for over a week now. Anna kept herself busy with spring cleaning. Mrs. Watson had everyone doing extra cleaning so that the hotel shined from top to bottom and from front to back, Anna would say to herself whenever her mind started to wonder. He will be back! She had just slipped the last hairpin into the bun on the back of her head when Seth softly knocked on her door. She opened her door and saw him standing there with a sheepish grin on his face. She wondered what he might be up to now.

He said quietly since it was very early and everyone else was asleep. "Thar's someone waiting down by the back door—wants ta see ya right away".

She rushed past Seth leaving him to close her door and she dashed down the hallway, down the stairs, through the kitchen and through the storage room. It was still pretty dark but she knew her way around. She lifted the latch on the backdoor and as she opened it, she saw him. Wes looked taller and older standing there in the early rays of this spring day. She jumped into his arms. He pulled her closer and held her tight. Then he kissed and kissed her almost like he could eat her up. When he stopped he held her away from him like he had to see if she was real. "I had to see ya fore I go to North Lake. I'll be back in time for the dance. Care ta go?"

Did she. She'd be ready to go anywhere with him where ever he said. Anna didn't have to answer. Her face told him all he needed to know.

"Now let me go. I've got to look after the horses."

Anna let her arms go limp to her sides. She watched him walk away and then she went into the kitchen to check on her mop water. Wesley was back. That is what mattered.

Seth came in the kitchen lugging two buckets of water. He set them down and than started chanting and walking around and around Anna. "Anna and a Wesley a kissing and a kissing. Soon there'll be babies a crying and a crying". Then he stopped and asked "When ya gittin married Anna?"

Anna picked up a towel and threw it at him. "You been a spying on me aye? Maybe I ought to box your ears like I see Mrs. Watson do". At that Seth turned sober and hurried to go get wood for the cook stove.

On the way to the dance Anna noticed that Wes was quiet. After, on their way to their favorite spot in the woods they rode along in silence. She could tell by the way his mustache twitched and he licked his lips that he had something bothering him. She wanted to ask but decided she'd let him tell her in his own time.

Wes stopped the horse. He turned, looked straight into her eyes and asked "Why don't you and me get hitched?"

She threw her arms around him saying, "Do you mean it Wes?" Then they were kissing and the way he was kissing, she just knew he meant it.

Wes was different. Ever since he had come back this spring Anna couldn't put it into words. She just felt it.

They picked up where they had left off last fall. Wes picked her up Saturday nights and they'd go to the dance and on Wednesdays they'd go for long walks. But when they were together, Wes seemed to be more intense in the way he treated her when they were alone.

Sometime in May Anna noticed that Wesley carried a bottle in the carriage. He started offering her a swig but she refused. The last of May turned very hot and even humid. It was exceptionally so and they were hot after the dance. Anna took him up on his offer. As they drove to their spot, they took turns having a swig. By the time Wes had stopped the horse and Anna had the blanket spread on the ground, they were both feeling relaxed. They lay together kissing and hugging as usual but this night there was no stopping their love making.

For the next few days Anna told herself it was alright what they had done. She loved Wesley and he loved her. After all, he had proposed marriage to her hadn't he?

Chapter 28

TIE THE KNOT?

Three weeks passed. The subject of marriage did not come up. Anna was feeling uneasy. She just had to know Wesley's intentions.

It was now late June. They were on their way to their favorite spot after the dance. Anna asked Wes if he would stop the horse.

Wes pulled back on the reins and Buckwheat immediately stopped.

"Now what's the matter? You've been tensed up like a frightened animal caught in a trap. Need a nip ta relax ya some?"

"NO! That's the last thing I want!" Anna snapped out at him. She took a breath and tried to say what was on her mind in a softer tone. She had to let Wesley know what she suspected. She would have felt better if she was 100 percent sure about this, but she had always been so regular. She was afraid. What would she do if Wesley refused to marry her? She chided herself for the thousandth time. How could she have been so careless to let this happen?

Anna wound her handkerchief around and around in her hands as she worked up courage to speak. She couldn't make herself look at him so she kept her eyes straight ahead as she began.

Quietly, she said, "Wes, were you serious, aye, when you asked about getting married?"

There! She had it out in the open. She had practiced how she would say it over and over all week in her head. She really hoped that he would not ask her why she was asking him. But, that's exactly what he did.

"Why are ye asking me that? Do ya think we shouldn't? Is there someone else ya want ta see?" Wesley's voice became louder and gruffer as he spoke. He seemed very agitated with her.

"NO!" she said trying to reassure him that is not why she had brought it up.

"There's no one. I need to know how you feel about it. About me," she said.

Before he could answer, she went on, "Do you remember the night I first drank from your bottle? I wish I hadn't. I had way too much that night and we..." She couldn't say more.

"What are ya saying?" Wes asked as he roughly took ahold of her shoulder and made her look at him. "Are ya asking me ta stop drinking?" He hurried on, "I won't! I like to drink. I like how it makes me feel. 'sides all the men I know drink, especially those at the lumbercamp. I won't give it up."

He didn't wait for her to answer. He took up the reins, slapped them on the rump of Buckwheat so suddenly that the horse jerked up his head and took off at a fast trot.

"Guess I'll be a getting ya back to the hotel."

Anna grabbed onto Wesley's arm. "No, Wes, please stop." Then, again asking him in a gentle voice, "please Wes, I need to ask you something more. It has nothing to do with you drinking." Anna still held tight to his arm imploring him to stop.

Wes pulled back on the reins and they stopped. He released the reins and set the break. Then he turned and looked at Anna.

Anna took a moment to swallow before asking, "Wes, do you love me, enough to marry me, aye?"

It was then that he relaxed. He took her hands in his and looking deeply into her eyes he answered. "Oh, if that's what's got ya all riled up tighter than a drum. I love ya. Alright, there ya got me ta say it to ya."

Anna pulled her hands away from his, looked straight ahead again, and began winding her hankerchief around and around in her hands. "It's just that I'm so worried. I'm late coming. What if I'm, I'm...." She couldn't bring herself to say carrying your child. She burst into tears and buried her face in her hankerchief.

Wes slid closer and held her and let her have her cry. He had had lots of practice seeing his sisters' cry. They'd be sobbing about something one minute and before anyone could turn around twice, they'd be laughing. Wes held her tight until she stopped shaking and had her tears under control. Then, he kissed her, took up the reins and headed Buckwheat back to town.

Neither of them spoke all the way back. Anna thought it best to let Wesley have time to think it over. She had said what she wanted him to know. Now, it would be up to him.

At the hotel, Wes tied Buckwheat to the post, helped Anna down from the carriage, and held her close to him as they walked around to the back door. He held her in his arms for a time, then kissed her on the lips and left.

Anna was glad for the darkness. She found her way easily through the kitchen and dining room and up the stairs. She had counted the steps many a time and knew exactly how many it took to reach her room. She closed her door and began undressing. She couldn't stop the tears. Kneeling down by her bed, she poured her heart out to God. She pleaded that he hear and help her, saying over and over did He forgive her for the mess she had gotten herself into? She bargained with God. If God saw to it that Wesley Stone marry her, she vowed she would stick by him no matter how hard their life might be. If she was with child, she pleaded to God that Wesley just had to marry her. She wanted this child to have both a mother and a father. Oh, God, she wasn't complaining about her Momma and Poppa Burns. They had been ever so good to her, but she hadn't forgotten the day she overheard that she was not a real Burns. As she recalled, Momma and she had gone to Grandma Burns' home and Anna had been sent out to gather all the firewood sticks she could find. She liked being outdoors rather than spending time inside with Grandma Burns. She couldn't have explained to anyone why she didn't like her Poppa's mother. The woman was nice enough to her when Momma was with her, but whenever Anna was left alone with the older woman, she was mean to Anna. It seemed to Anna that Grandma made her work awfully hard and if Anna didn't do it the way she insisted, or she thought Anna wasn't working fast enough, Grandma hit her with the stick that she always had with her to help get her out of a chair or get around in the house. That day, as she came close to the outside door with her arms full of firewood, she could hear loud talking. Grandma was yelling at Momma. Grandma Burns was saying something about how Momma and Poppa had taken in that girl. Anna didn't know at first who they were talking about, but as she crept closer to the door, she could hear better. She heard about how they had taken in a girl and her baby, how they had given the girl all their savings and sent her away, keeping the baby. Grandma's voice got even louder as she went on raving about how they had named the baby after her, Bridget Burns. Momma kept trying to quiet Grandma but she kept raving. Anna didn't stick around to listen to any more. She dropped her bundle of wood and fled to the woods. She ran until she couldn't catch her breath. She slid down the side of a large tree and sobbed her heart out.

Anna never knew how long she stayed out there. When she stopped crying, she made up her mind that she'd go home and never tell what she had overheard. She made up her mind that that old lady would not know what she had heard her say. She loved her Momma and Poppa and she knew they loved her, as if she was their real own little girl. But, she didn't have to like Grandma Burns!

Momma was calling her. She hurried back. They walked home hand in hand. As they walked, Anna told Momma how she had spent most of her day chasing a baby squirrel. She never caught it and it climbed up a tree where she saw another squirrel above chattering and chattering at her.

Chapter 29

WESLEY

He tossed and turned. He beat his fists into the pillow. He turned the pillow over and beat the other side. What Annie has said raced around in his head. She was carrying his child. Was he going to marry her?

It was hot. He threw the coverlet from him. He got out of bed and paced the floor. He laid back down. What would he do? He knew what he should do but did he want to be married?

It flitted in his mind. He could leave and go back home to Canada. No, he wouldn't do that. There wasn't anything in Flinton for him. Besides, he didn't want to go crawling back home. He didn't want to ask his brother, Hawley, for a job. There wasn't anything left in Flinton to do but work for Hawley. He owned the store, the livery such as it was with renting out an occasional carriage or sled, or else help his Dad make caskets, when necessary. The mine was shut down and logging was becoming scarce, except for cutting firewood for people. No, there was nothing he wanted to do in Flinton.

He sat up. He had made a life for himself here in Forestport. It had taken him over three years to get this far and here is where he'd stay. No going home, except maybe some day to visit. He did miss his mother. When he had first come to America, he worked for one logging outfit or another but not staying with any for very long. Then, he landed this job, driving for C.J.Brookstead, at the livery here in Forestport. Then there was Connie Breen. Connie depended on him, especially since the train accident. Connie was crippled and unable to care for his horses. They needed him and he liked the feeling of them depending on him. Then, in winter, he enjoyed working on Beaver River at the logging camp. He felt like he was needed, liked and belonged with the rest of those kind of rough outdoorsmen who worked long, hard hours in the woods. He enjoyed quiet times with them drinking and smoking or chewing tobacco. He was quite proud of this life he had carved out for himself.

But now, what about Annie? Admittedly, he had asked her to marry him. He had thought someday, they would get hitched, but not so soon. He wasn't ready. That wasn't part of his plan. Maybe a few years from now. What she said tonight changed everything.

Stella. Why did she come to his mind? He had had to push all thoughts of Stella out of his heart and mind. He had loved her, or at least he thought it was love. Stella was gone, gone from Forestport, gone from him. Her mother said she had no plans to ever come back to Forestport. She was traveling further and further west. He had best forget about her, that's just what her mother had told him. That had not been easy to do. He had really tried and done quite well, up till tonight.

What was he to do about Annie? Annie was here. She was steady. He knew she had eyes only for him, not like Stella. Stella was one for talking up to any man. She was restless. She always talked to him about moving out west and seeing the world.

He had more in common with Annie. Annie was here in Forestport. As far as Wesley could tell, Annie was happy to be living here. Both of them were from Canada. They were from small hamlets. They weren't consumed with wanting to live in any big city or felt the need to move out west. They were country people.

Annie was pretty with her brown hair and brown eyes that could snap at you if you startled her or if she was out of sorts with you about something. Annie was a good cook. She enjoyed her work at the hotel. She talked about sensible things, not about women's clothes or the need to have the latest hat from New York City. She listened when he talked about his work with the horses. Yes. Wes felt comfortable around Annie. They did have more in common, when he took time to think about it.

Wesley guessed he did love Annie. He had told her so, didn't he? Didn't that mean he meant it? Besides, when you got to the real issue, it was just as much his fault as hers if she was carrying his child. Well, that settled it! They had to get married.

Wesley lay back down and was soon sound asleep. He had made up his mind. First chance he got tomorrow, he'd start making plans-plans for Annie and him.

Chapter 30

WAITING

The next day was Sunday. Anna was glad to walk with Clara to church. Maybe God would be able to hear her better in church. She'd ask HIM again about Wes marrying her. He just had to.

Anna went through the rituals of the service out of sheer habit. She certainly didn't hear anything the priest was saying. Her mind was too occupied with praying for herself.

On their way to the hotel after church, Anna was quiet. Usually she was chattering an ear off Clara, but today they walked in silence. As they rounded the curve in the road and were in view of the hotel, Clara noticed it first and pointed it out to Anna.

"Isn't that the rig your Wesley Stone picks you up in on Saturday nights?" Clara asked.

Anna had been walking with her eyes down cast, staring at the dirt road, but her head jerked up at Clara's question. Yes, it sure looked like the same one. Anna wanted to break into a run but she held herself in check. Her mind was racing though. Was it really Wesley? Why was he here on a Sunday morning? Was he here to tell her goodbye? If that was the reason, she couldn't face him. She'd start crying all over again.

As they approached, she saw it was Wes. He was standing in front of Buckwheat, stroking the horse's face. Wesley looked up and noticed Anna and Clara and he broke into a smile.

"Mornin." he said addressing his remark towards Clara. She returned his greeting and went up the step and into the hotel. He called out to Anna.

"Annie, I need ta speak ta ya," Anna walked to the front of the horse while searching Wes' face, trying to read it.

Wesley continued, "I spoke to Mr. Watson. He gave ya the day off. Mrs. Watson made us some sandwiches. Thought we might take a ride."

Anna's face lit up. "I'll just be a minute." Anna took off almost at a run, up the step and into the hotel. She took two stair steps at a time and did run to her room. She didn't care how unladylike she looked. She didn't take time to hang up her church dress but flung it on the bed, grabbed her everyday dress slipping it over her head and reaching for her everyday shoes. She didn't even fasten them up. Taking the shawl off the door hook and closing her door, she ran back down the stairs and outdoors before Seth could stop her to ask questions. He came out of the kitchen as she went whizzing by.

Wesley helped her up into the carriage and hurried around to take his seat beside her. Buckwheat seemed to sense their urgency and stepped lively as Wesley directed him in a totally new direction. Anna didn't even think to question where they were headed. She didn't care. She was so glad to be with Wes. He had come for her and that had to mean he wasn't going to abandon her or their baby.

Wesley drove north and didn't stop until they came to a small lake. Wes tied Buckwheat to a small tree while Anna spread a blanket on the ground. What a lovely place for a picnic.

As they ate their sandwiches, Anna glanced every few minutes at Wesley. She tried to read the expression on his face. So far they hadn't said anything of importance to each other. They finished eating and sat close together enjoying the day. Wesley asked, "Have ya told anyone what ya suspect?"

"No." Anna said. "Why are you asking me that, aye?"

"Well, while I was waiting for ya, Mr. Watson handed me the picnic basket and said he hoped that I'd be doing right by ya."

"Mr. Watson is a caring man. He worries about me like I was one of his own daughters. That's all."

"Well," Wesley said, "Do we have ta get married?"

"NO!" Anna said getting herself off the blanket as she continued on, "We don't have to get married!" Anna was not liking this. It wasn't how she hoped the day would turn out. She gathered up the basket and started walking fast towards the carriage.

Wesley stood up and reached out to catch her arm, "What are ya doing?" he asked her as he made her face him, "What are ya getting so upset about?"

She looked straight into his eyes as she spoke, "If you don't want to marry me, Wesley Stone, you don't have to. I am carrying your child but I will raise it by myself. You needn't feel that you have to marry me!" By now she was at the verge of tears. She looked away before he saw the tears forming in her eyes.

At that, he turned her around towards him. Taking her by the elbows and again making her face him. "Look at me!" Then softer he added, "Annie, I never said I didn't want ta marry ya."

She looked up at him saying almost in a mere whisper, "Well, you didn't say you wanted to either, aye?"

"Well, I do want ta marry ya." he retorted. Tears fell as he held her close to him. This time she was crying from relief and joy. He handed her his handkerchief. When she was composed, he kissed her again and again and told her he loved her and wanted to marry her soon.

When Wesley left her at the hotel back door, he said that he would make all the arrangements. She was to be ready when he came for her.

Chapter 31

THE WEDDING

July 4, 1898 arrived. Anna was ready. She awoke extra early but couldn't stay in bed. After several silent prayers, she dressed in her wedding attire, except for her gloves. She put them in her new purse along with a new handkerchief. Thanks to the Watson's, Clara and Seth, she was outfitted in all new clothes befitting a wedding day.

It was early so she had plenty of time to spend arranging her hair. The hairpins just didn't want to cooperate but finally she was well pleased. She pinned her new hat on top of her head, checking in the mirror to be sure it was as she wanted. Before leaving the room to go have a bite of breakfast, she remembered what Seth had said last night, "Somethin old, somethin new, somethin borrowered, and somethin blue." She had it all covered thanks to her friends. She felt satisfied she was ready to get married to Wesley Stone today. She closed her eyes and said a prayer of thanks to God for making it all possible.

In the kitchen she found Seth was up and filling the water reservoir on the cook stove. She set to frying eggs for herself and Seth. She was about to put the last bite into her mouth when they heard a knocking on the front door. Seth went to see if it was Wes while Anna took care of their dishes. It was indeed Wes. Anna had never seen him so dressed up. He had on a three piece black suit, a new grey hat and shiny new black shoes. She was so proud of him. How handsome he was. He walked over to her, "Are ya ready?"

"Aye." was all she squeaked out. "Let's be off!" he said as he took ahold of her elbow.

"Wait," Anna said, "Seth would you please get my two satchels from my room?"

Seth helped them get settled in the carriage and waved a goodbye. Anna couldn't have felt any happier. She wrapped her arm around Wes's as he held the reins and they were on their way.

Wes was feeling good about the day, too. Anna noticed how talkative he was all the way to Boonville. She sat and listened as he filled her in on all the arrangements he had made. The sun shone brightly as they came closer and closer to Boonville. Anna took that for a good sign from God. She whispered to Wes, "I am so happy. I promise I will stay by you like you stuck by me, aye? I love you."

Wesley squeezed her hand, "And I love ya, too."

Before long, they were in Boonville. Wesley was somewhat familiar with it having made a few deliveries from time to time for the Forestport livery. In fact, his friend, James Darrow, worked at the Booneville livery all summer and logged in the woods with Wesley in the winter. James was to be his best man today.

As they passed the Catholic Church, Anna felt a twinge in her stomach. She had always thought she would someday be married in the church. Momma had told her many a time how she and Poppa had been married in a small Catholic Church in Ireland before they crossed the Atlantic Ocean to Canada. But, Wes had made it abundantly clear to her he had no intention of being married in a Catholic Church. She gave a quick prayer asking God to forgive her.

Wes drove into a wide driveway leading up to a large two story beautiful, grand house. He told her they were being married by Judge Whitcomb. She had never imagined how fine a home it would be. She waited while Wes tied Buckwheat to the shiny black iron post at the edge of a well groomed side walk. Then he came and helped her down. She used her hands to smooth any wrinkles in her dress. Wes took her by the elbow and led her up the walkway and onto a wraparound porch. She began to feel butterflies jumping around in her stomach as they came to the fancy glassed front door. Wesley rapped on the door using the brass knocker. He removed his hat and held it nervously in his hands. After what seemed a long time, a grey haired, stocky woman wearing a plain gray dress and black laced shoes opened the door a crack.

"May I help you?" she asked as she looked from Wesley to Anna and back to Wesley.

Anna let Wes do the talking. Wes answered, "Is the judge here?"

"Yes," she said nodding her head up and down as she opened the door wide. "Come in and I'll get him for you." When they were inside she added, "Wait right here."

She closed the door behind them. Anna surveyed the room. She could tell it was furnished with expensive furniture and much fancier than she had ever seen. There was an unusually long sofa facing a large stone fireplace directly in front of them with several matching chairs on each side, making a semi circle. Behind the sofa and near to them was a long and well polished wooden table. On the table there was a collection of fancy dishes. Anna wanted so much to pick each one up to give it a closer look and admire its beauty. She knew better and put her hands down by her sides so she wouldn't be so tempted. She used her eyes to wander the rest of the room. She looked at the windows. They seemed to run from ceiling to floor with a deep blue velvet material in panels on each side held by gold rope ties. In front of each window was a small table with sitting chairs on each side. On the wall to their left, was gold trimmed full length mirror and marble shelf at the bottom with a small tuft footstool underneath. Anna had begun to study the other wall to their right when a tall, distinguished looking man walked briskly towards them. He stretched his hand out to Wes. Wes shook hands as the man called him, 'Stoney'

"I hope we're not too early, judge." The judge replied, "Not at all." Then looking at Anna he said, "This must be the bride."

Wes spoke up, "This is Annie."

"You're face looks familiar. Haven't I seen you somewhere?" Before Anna could answer he went on, "Are you from Boonville? Maybe, I know your folks."

Anna shook her head as Wesley explained that Anna used to work at the Hulbert House.

"Sure enough. That's it. That's where I've seen you. But, I don't believe I've seen you there lately, have I?"

Again Wesley answered for her, saying, that Anna had moved to Forestport and worked at the Buffalo Head Hotel, now.

"The mystery is solved. You two have come here to be married. But first, I must tell you, Annie, that this man you are about to yoke yourself to for life, is a good man. He came to my rescue one snowy night over a year ago. I had been trying a case way up north and I was on my way home after dark when I suddenly got caught in a blizzard. My poor horse, buggy, and I were stranded in a deep snowdrift. This fine young man comes driving along and finds us. He was driving a team of stocky horses who were pulling a full load of firewood. Why, he just pulled us out of that drift in a matter of minutes. I think I could have gotten myself home from there but your man here insisted that I follow his tracks. I am sure he went way out of his way to be sure that I got safely home. As I recall, he even took time to put my horse in the barn out back and rubbed him down. Then, he left, refusing to take a cent for his troubles. So, today, I am honored to have you be married in my home. And, I will be paying the parson."

He turned to Wesley. "The minister, pastor Dunbane, a good man, will be here shortly to do the marrying. Also, James Darrow. I did contact John Bellinger, like you asked, but have not heard whether his wife, Flora was it?" He turned to Anna, "Will be able to come. But, never you mind, my housekeeper, Mrs. Meeks is prepared and more than willing to stand up with you."

Anna's heart skipped a beat. Oh, she hoped with all her heart that her dearest friend, Flora, would be coming to stand up with her.

120

There was a knock and Mrs. Meeks opened the door. Anna caught sight of Flora and nearly flew to her. Anna hugged Flora who had her hands full of fresh cut flowers. Mrs. Meeks led the two girls down a hallway and into a spacious kitchen. Flora laid the flowers carefully on the table. Then she wrapped her arms around Anna. The two of them clung to each other with tears running down both their cheeks.

Flora held Anna out at arm's length, "Let me look at you. What a lovely bride you make. So pretty in your wedding dress and all. Let's get to making you a bouquet to hold. I picked these right from my own yard." Flora said proudly.

"Oh Flora," Anna said as she took out her handkerchief to dab at her face. "I am so very glad you came. I might have known you would bring flowers. Thank you."

It didn't take Flora long to break off extra long stems and fashion the white and yellow and blue into a bouquet tied with some white ribbon she had brought along. She handed it to Anna.

"Now, I shall make a smaller one for me to hold on this especial day."

Anna stood and marveled as her friend made it look so easy. "Flora, I had forgotten how much you enjoy flowers and what a talent you have with them."

"Oh shaw, Anna, 'tis nothing more than you do with thread and needle. I have watched you crochet flowers. I grow them and you make them. Just in two different ways, but just as beautiful. There! Now, I am ready to meet your husband to be. Let's go."

They found the men all gathered near a desk. One man was seated. Anna guessed him to be the pastor. He was busy writing. Judge Whitcomb noticed the ladies and motioned for them to join the men at the desk. "This is Reverend Dunbane. Reverend Dunbane this is Annie Burns and her friend, Flora Bellinger."
Reverend Dunbane remained seated. He continued to write on a

paper as he asked questions and received an answer. Then he had Wes sign his name as groom, Anna sign as the bride, James as the best man and Flora as maid of honor. When all had signed, Judge Whitcomb took charge arranging each in proper standing order in front of the fireplace.

Wes took hold of Anna's hand as they stood facing Reverend Dunbane. Flora was on Anna's left and James was on Wes' right. The judge and Mrs. Meeks stood behind them. Anna could feel Wes' hand twitch and she knew he was as nervous as she. The pastor asked them to repeat after him and somehow the vows got said out loud. It was all over in a matter of minutes but it felt longer to Anna. Wes gave her a quick kiss on the lips and then Flora was a hugging both of them. The others followed suit with the judge slapping Wes on the back with hardy congratulations.

Reverend Dunbane handed the signed papers to Wes, saying congratulations to Mr. and Mrs. Stone before he quickly left wishing them a long and happy life. The judge insisted the rest of them stay for a wedding toast. Mrs. Meeks hurried to the kitchen and came back carrying a silver tray with tall stemmed glasses on it. The judge took a bottle of wine from a cupboard near the fireplace. He poured some into each glass and Mrs. Meeks passed one to each of them. Judge Whitcomb gave a rather lengthy toast and they clicked glasses together before drinking. James looked at his watch and said he must hurry away. His special girl had a 4th of July picnic planned and he had promised not to be late meeting her. Flora said she must get home and rescue John from little Johnny, plus she had more preparations to do before the picnic she had planned for all of them.

Wes thanked the judge for everything and said they had to be going. Anna wanted to spend some time at the Hulbert House before joining the Bellinger's picnic. As they walked down the sidewalk, Wes said, "So, how do you feel being Mrs. Annie Stone?" Anna couldn't begin to tell how grateful she felt. She now had a legal name.

From now on she would be Mrs. Anna B. Stone.

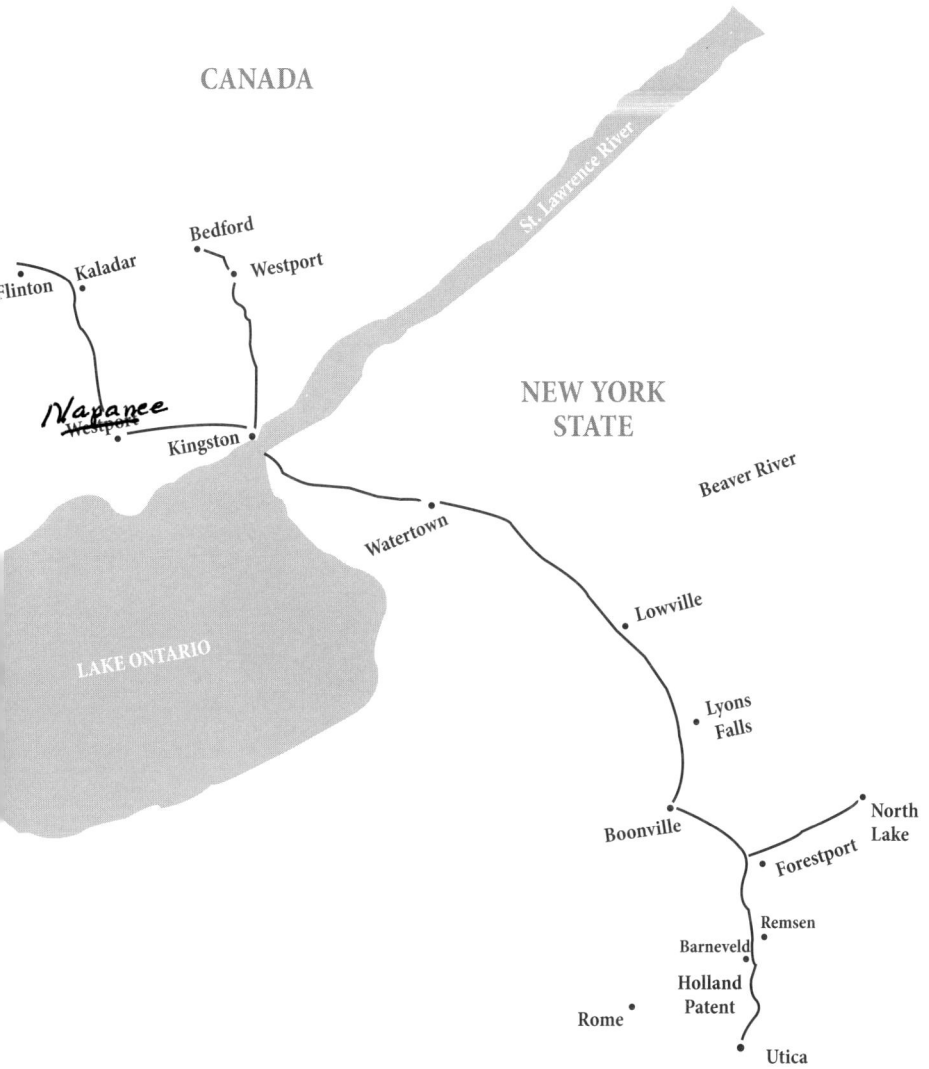

Thomas Wesley Stone
February 14, 1874 - April 20, 1938
64 Years Old

Flinton, Ontario
Canada

Sherrill,
Oneida, New York

Anna Burns Stone
January 22, 1880 - August 7, 1955
75 Years Old

Bedford, Ontario
Canada

Sherrill,
Oneida, New York

CERTIFICATE AND RECORD OF MARRIAGE

STATE OF NEW YORK—BUREAU OF VITAL STATISTICS.

Registered No. 11701

Date of Marriage.	July 4, 1848
Groom's Full Name.	Kiraby Stone
Residence of Groom.	Frankfort
Age.	23
Color.	White
Occupation.	Laborer
Single or Widowed.	Single
Birthplace of Groom.	Canada
Father's Name.	Joseph Stone
Mother's Maiden Name.	Arhranda Masers
Number of Groom's Marriage.	First
Bride's Full Name.	Anna Burns
Residence of Bride.	Frankfort
Age.	18
Color.	White
Single or Widowed.	Single
Maiden Name, if a Widow.	
Birthplace of Bride.	Canada
Father's Name.	Peter Burns
Mother's Maiden Name.	Mary McAllister
Number of Bride's Marriage.	First
Name of Person performing Cer'mony	A. G. Dunham
Official Station.	Clergyman
Residence.	Boonville
Date of Local Registration.	July 5, 1898

FOR GENEALOGICAL RESEARCH ONLY

I Hereby Certify, that

were joined in Marriage

by me in accordance with the laws of the State of New York, at Boonville, N.Y.

this ____ day of July 1898

FOR GENEALOGICAL RESEARCH ONLY

We, the Groom and Bride named in this Certificate, hereby certify, that the information given therein is correct, to the best of our knowledge and belief.

Wesley Mona .... Groom.

Emma Emma .... Bride.

Signed in the presence of

James B Darrow

and

Flora E Billings